CHRISTMAS CARAMEL MURDER

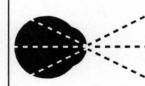

This Large Print Book carries the
Seal of Approval of N.A.V.H.

CHRISTMAS CARAMEL MURDER

JOANNE FLUKE

THORNDIKE PRESS
A part of Gale, Cengage Learning

 GALE
CENGAGE Learning®

Farmington Hills, Mich • San Francisco • New York • Waterville, Maine
Meriden, Conn • Mason, Ohio • Chicago

GALE
CENGAGE Learning®

Copyright © 2016 by H. L. Swenson, Inc.
A Hannah Swenson Mystery with Recipes.
Thorndike Press, a part of Gale, Cengage Learning.

ALL RIGHTS RESERVED
Thorndike Press® Large Print Mystery.
The text of this Large Print edition is unabridged.
Other aspects of the book may vary from the original edition.
Set in 16 pt. Plantin.

LIBRARY OF CONGRESS CATALOGING-IN-PUBLICATION DATA

Names: Fluke, Joanne, 1943- author.
Title: Christmas caramel murder / Joanne Fluke.
Description: Large print edition. | Waterville, Maine : Thorndike Press, 2016. |
    Series: A Hannah Swensen mystery with recipes | Series: Thorndike Press large
    print mystery
Identifiers: LCCN 2016036049 | ISBN 9781410492463 (hardback) | ISBN 141049246X
    (hardcover)
Subjects: LCSH: Swensen, Hannah (Fictitious character)—Fiction. | Bakers—Fiction. |
    Women detectives—Fiction. | Murder—Investigation—Fiction. | Large type
    books. | BISAC: FICTION / Mystery & Detective / General. | GSAFD: Mystery
    fiction.
Classification: LCC PS3556.L685 C49 2016 | DDC 813/.54—dc23
LC record available at https://lccn.loc.gov/2016036049

Published in 2016 by arrangement with Kensington Books, an imprint
of Kensington Publishing Corp.

This book is for lovely Frida Giselle.

ACKNOWLEDGEMENTS:

Big hugs to the kids and the grandkids.

Thank you to my friends and neighbors: Mel & Kurt, Lyn & Bill, Gina, Dee Appleton, Jay, Richard Jordan, Laura Levine, the real Nancy and Heiti, Dr. Bob & Sue, Dan, Mark & Mandy at Faux Library, Daryl and her staff at Groves Accountancy, Gene and Ron at SDSA, and everyone at Boston Private Bank.

Thanks to Brad, Stephanie, Eric, Amanda, Lorenzo, Nancey, Meg, Bruce, Alison, Cameron, Gabriel, Barbara, and everyone at the Hallmark Movies & Mysteries Channel who gave us the Murder She Baked Hannah Swensen movies. What fun to see Hannah on TV!

Thank you to my Minnesota friends: Lois & Neal, Bev & Jim, Lois & Jack, Val,

Ruthann, Lowell, Dorothy & Sue, Mary & Jim, Pat and Gary at their Once Upon a Crime Bookstore, and Tim Hedges.

A grateful hug to my multi-talented friend and Editor-in-Chief, John Scognamiglio.

Thanks to all the wonderful folks at Kensington Publishing who keep Hannah sleuthing and baking up a storm.

Thanks to Meg Ruley and the staff at the Jane Rotrosen Agency for their constant support and their wise advice.

Thanks to Hiro Kimura, my wonderful cover artist for the incredibly delicious-looking caramels on this book cover. My caramels don't come close to looking this delectable, but they *do* taste better!

Thank you to Lou Malcangi at Kensington Publishing, for designing all of Hannah's deliciously stunning covers.

Thanks to John at *Placed4Success.com* for Hannah's movie and TV placements, his presence on all of Hannah's social media, the countless hours he puts in on my behalf, and for always being there for me.

Thanks to Rudy for maintaining my website at **wwwJoanneFluke.com**, his talent behind the camera, and for giving support to Hannah's social media.

Big thanks to Kathy Allen for the final testing of every single one of Hannah's recipes.

Hugs to Judy Q. for helping with Hannah's e-mail at **Gr8Clues@JoanneFluke.com** and searching for answers to research questions.

Grateful hugs to my super friend, Trudi Nash, for going on book tours with me, for keeping me on an even keel, and for thinking of new and innovative recipe ideas for us to try.

Thanks to food stylist and media guide extraordinaire Lois Brown for her friendship and her talented assistance.

Hugs to the Double D's, Alicia, Fern, Leah, and everyone on Team Swensen who helps to keep Hannah's Facebook presence alive and well.

Thank you to Dr. Rahhal, Dr. and Cathy Line, Dr. Wallen. Dr. Koslowski, Drs. Ashley and Lee, and Dr. Niemeyer (*who reminds me of Doc Knight*) for putting up with my pesky Hannah-book-related medical and dental questions. Norman and Doc Knight would be lost without you!

Grateful thanks to all of the Hannah fans who share their favorite family recipes with me, post on Facebook, watch the Hannah movies, and devour each and every book. I hope you love reading Christmas Caramel Murder just as much as I loved writing it.

PROLOGUE

The dining room at the Lake Eden Inn was festive with corn shocks, hay bales, pumpkins, and giant beer steins made of papier-mâché. It was clear that the owners, Sally and Dick Laughlin, were getting ready for their Oktoberfest celebration over the weekend.

It was Thursday night, and Hannah Swensen smiled at Ross Barton as she finished the last delicious bite of her dinner. "That was wonderful. Thank you, Ross."

Sally, who was waiting on them personally, must have had a version of dessert radar because she approached just as soon as Hannah placed her flatware on the plate.

"I've got a new dessert for you to try," Sally announced, motioning to the nearest busboy to clear their plates. When there was room to display it, she placed a large silver dessert tray on the table.

"Something for Oktoberfest?" Hannah

asked her.

"No, for Christmas. I decided to feature chocolate and caramel, the way you did in the children's gift bags last year. That's why I'm featuring chocolate flan with caramel whipped cream."

"I've never heard of caramel whipped cream before," Hannah told her.

"It's easy to make. I couldn't find a recipe, but I followed your advice. We were talking about recipes and you said, *'If you can't find a recipe, make one up.'* So that's exactly what I did."

"And it worked?"

"Not the first time, and not the second time, either. But I revised it again, and the third time was the charm. I tried it out on Dick first, and he said he loves it. The only problem is, Dick has a sweet tooth and he loves everything I bake. I'd really like to try it out on you if you'll promise to tell me exactly what you think."

"It looks wonderful!" Hannah said, watching as Sally cut two slices from the flan that was sitting in the center of the silver tray and placed them in crystal dessert dishes. She added several dollops of caramel whipped cream, and placed the dessert dishes in front of Hannah and Ross.

"Be honest," she warned them. "And be

critical, too. Tell me if I need to add something to make it better."

Hannah and Ross picked up their dessert spoons and took bites almost simultaneously. Then both of them smiled.

"Delicious!" Hannah declared.

"Oh, yes!" Ross concurred, taking another bite. "The chocolate is really rich, and it's perfect with the caramel whipped cream."

"Thanks!" Sally said, looking relieved as she turned to Hannah. "I'm still trying to figure out how to decorate this flan to make it even more Christmassy."

"It looks great just the way it is," Hannah told her, "but it could be more festive for Christmas. I'll let you know if I think of anything. And I'll ask Lisa. She's my decorating expert."

"Just one more thing," Sally said, picking up the platter. "What do you think I should call it?"

"Call it exactly what it is," Hannah suggested. "Chocolate Flan with Caramel Whipped Cream. If you call it something else, your wait staff will have to answer questions about what it is."

Sally nodded. "That's a really good point. Thanks for the help and enjoy the rest of your dessert."

When Sally had left their table, Ross

13

turned to Hannah. "I've never tasted Lisa's chocolate caramels. Are you making them for Christmas this year?"

"Only if you really want us to," Hannah said, frowning slightly. "I know it's silly to be superstitious, but . . . well . . . they were bad luck last year."

"What do you mean?"

"I mean, last Christmas was . . . pretty strange in the giant scheme of things. You weren't here, so you wouldn't know, but something bad happened with the caramels."

"Something bad?"

"Yes. I found some of them at a murder scene."

"Tell me all about it." Ross leaned forward and covered Hannah's hand with his.

"Well . . ." Hannah drew a deep breath. "This is going to take a while. It's a really long story."

Ross glanced at his watch. "That's okay. It's only six-thirty. What time does Sally close the dining room?"

"She's open until ten." Hannah was silent for a moment, and then she looked amused. "It could take almost that long to tell you. Are you sure you want to listen to a long story now?"

"I'm positive. You've got me curious,

Cookie. Tell me."

"Okay." Hannah gave a mock sigh. "Just remember, you asked for it. But first, we'll need more coffee."

Hannah waited until one of the waitresses had brought a fresh carafe of coffee, and then she began her story.

"It was the first Monday in December, and Lisa and I were in the coffee shop at The Cookie Jar. It was early, an hour before we were due to open, and we were decorating for Christmas. We were almost finished when everything started to happen. . . ."

CHOCOLATE FLAN WITH
CARAMEL WHIPPED CREAM

Preheat oven to 350 degrees F., rack in the middle position.

For the Chocolate Flan:
1 and 3/4 cup whole milk
1 cup (*6-ounce by weight bag*) semi-sweet chocolate chips (*I used Ghirardelli*)
4 large eggs
1 can (*14 ounces*) sweetened condensed milk (*I used Eagle Brand*)
1 teaspoon vanilla extract
1/2 teaspoon salt
chocolate curls for a topping are optional (*Make them by scraping them from a dark chocolate bar with the blade of a sharp knife.*)

For the Caramel Whipped Cream:
1 cup whipping cream
5 Tablespoons caramel ice cream topping (*I used Smucker's*)

Select a round glass casserole that's approximately 10 inches in diameter.

Locate a baking pan with 4-inch or taller sides that is large enough to hold your glass casserole with at least an inch and a half of space on all sides.

Set the casserole you've chosen inside the baking pan. Eventually, this baking pan will hold hot water to "bathe" the outside of your flan casserole. This water bath, or **bain marie**, will keep your flan from baking too rapidly and becoming hard around the edges.

Spray the inside of the glass casserole with Pam or another nonstick cooking spray.

Hannah's 1st Note: Don't use anything called "baking" spray on the inside of your casserole. It contains flour and you don't want flour on the outside of your flan.

Put two potholders or oven mitts out on the counter where they will be handy.

Heat the cup and three-quarters of whole milk at MEDIUM heat on the stovetop in a medium-size saucepan until it almost comes to a boil. You'll be able to tell this is going to happen when bubbles start to form around the edges of the saucepan and steam begins to escape from the milk.

Pull the saucepan with the milk over to a cold stovetop burner and stir in the cup of semi-sweet chocolate chips.

Stir until the chips are melted and the mixture is a uniform color. If this doesn't happen, your milk was too cold. Put it back on the burner and stir constantly for another minute to make sure the chips are melted. Then pull it off the heat and turn off the stovetop burner.

In a large bowl on the counter, whisk the 4 large eggs until they're light-colored and fluffy.

Hannah's 2nd Note: You can also do this in the bowl of an electric mixer.

Add the can of sweetened condensed milk, the vanilla extract, and the salt to the bowl with the eggs.

Whisk the contents until they're well incorporated.

Carefully, feel the outside of the saucepan with the chocolate mixture. If it's not so hot that it will cook the eggs, slowly, add the chocolate mixture to the egg mixture. Whisk or beat until everything is well incorporated.

Pour the resulting mixture into your prepared casserole.

Set your casserole inside the larger baking pan.

Run water as hot as you can get from your tap, and fill a large measuring cup with a spout.

Pour hot water from the measuring cup inside the larger pan. Keep pouring until the water level reaches halfway up the sides of the casserole holding your flan.

Loosely cover your flan with foil and poke

a few holes in the foil to let steam escape as it's baking.

Carry both pans to the oven and put them inside to bake.

Bake your flan at 350 degrees F. for 50 to 70 minutes, or until the blade of a table knife inserted one inch from the center of the flan comes out clean.

Hannah's 3rd Note: If your knife has liquid residue sticking to it when you remove it, your flan is not fully baked. Give it another 5 minutes in the oven, wash and dry your table knife in the meantime, and test it again.

When your table knife comes out clean, use oven potholders to take both pans out of the oven together and set them on a cold stovetop burner.

Use potholders or oven mitts to lift out the inner casserole with your flan and place it on a second cold burner or on a wire rack. Use potholders or oven mitts to dump out the water in the outer pan and set it aside to cool.

Set your timer for 20 minutes.

When your Chocolate Caramel Flan has cooled for 20 minutes, cover the top of the flan casserole with plastic wrap. Refrigerate your flan in the casserole for at least 4 hours, or until it's time to serve dessert.

Overnight is fine too, if you want to make it the day before you plan to serve it.

To serve, run a table knife around the inside rim of your flan to loosen it slightly. Turn it out in a flat bowl or onto a plate with a deep lip. Then make the Caramel Whipped Cream.

In the bowl of an electric mixer, mix the cup of whipping cream and the 5 Tablespoons of caramel ice cream topping together.

Gradually, increase the speed of the mixer to MEDIUM-HIGH and beat until the resulting mixture will hold a soft peak. (*Test for soft peaks by shutting off the mixer and dipping the flat blade of a rubber spatula into the whipped cream and pulling it up quickly. If it forms a peak, but the tip droops slightly, you have achieved soft peaks.*)

"Frost" your flan with the Caramel Whipped Cream. People will ooh and ahh when you cut slices, place them in dessert dishes and serve it.

Hannah's 4th Note: If you want to make your dessert really fancy, garnish the slices with chocolate curls and extra caramel whipped cream.

Yield: This Chocolate Flan with Caramel Whipped Cream serves 6 to 8 people unless you invite Andrea's husband, Bill. Bill is absolutely crazy for this dessert. He boasted to me that he could eat a whole flan all by himself, and I believe him.

CHAPTER ONE

"I'd better steady the ladder for you," Hannah warned as Lisa picked up the star ornament that fit on the very top of their Christmas tree and climbed up the first rung. "Are you sure you want to go do this? I really meant to get a new ladder after last year, but I forgot."

"That's understandable. The only time we use a ladder is at Christmas. But don't worry, Hannah. I can do it. I'm not afraid of heights, at least not usually."

"But you are right now?" Hannah asked, hearing the slight quaver in her young partner's voice.

"I'm a *little* nervous, that's all. It's just that the top of our tree seems like a long ways up."

"You're right, Lisa It *is* way up there. We got a sixteen-foot tree this year."

"I know, but it didn't seem this tall at the Christmas tree lot."

"That's probably because it was flanked by two blue spruces that were taller."

"How tall were those?"

"They were twenty-footers, and this one would have looked a lot shorter in comparison."

"I'm glad we didn't get a twenty-footer!" Lisa gave a little laugh. "I know it's impossible, but this tree looks like it's growing taller by the minute."

Lisa climbed up another rung. Then she reached down to hand Hannah the star tree-topper. "Will you hold this until I get about halfway up? I want to hold on to this ladder with both hands."

"No problem. Just let me know when you want the tree-topper and I'll give it to you."

Hannah held the ornament with one hand while she steadied the ladder with the other. The ladder wobbled, and she wished she'd remembered to shop for a new one.

Lisa climbed up the fourth rung and looked at the top of the tree again. "Let's get a shorter tree next year."

"We will. I promise."

"And a new ladder."

"That, too. I'll call Cliff at the hardware store right after we're through decorating the tree."

"Sounds good." Lisa climbed up another

rung, and then she stopped. "I'm almost up high enough. Hand me the tree-topper, Hannah. I'll bend down."

"And I'll stretch up." Hannah reached up with her right hand, but she kept her left hand firmly on the ladder. "Here you go, Lisa."

Lisa bent down even farther and grabbed the ornament. "Got it!" she said, straightening up again and reaching toward the top of the tree.

At that precise moment, the back door opened and a familiar voice shouted, "Girls! Come quick! It's an emergency!"

The ladder wobbled as Hannah reacted to the panic in her mother's voice. Lisa let out a little gasp of fright, but somehow she managed to attach the tree-topper and climb down two rungs before the ladder began to tip.

"I can't hold it!" Hannah exclaimed as the ladder tipped even further. "Jump, Lisa!"

Lisa didn't wait for a second invitation. She leaped down to the floor as the ladder collapsed with a clatter of old wood and stressed metal fasteners as it fell apart.

"Good heavens! What on earth happened?"

Hannah and Lisa turned to see Delores

25

Swensen standing in the doorway, staring at them in shock. "And where did you get that decrepit old ladder?"

"It was Dad's," Hannah said, resisting the urge to rail at her mother for startling them at such a critical point in their decorating endeavor. She took a deep breath to calm down, and then she asked, "What's the emergency, Mother?"

"Perhaps I shouldn't have used the word *emergency* to describe it," Delores replied, sounding slightly contrite. And then, in typical Delores fashion, she changed the subject. "How did you get Dad's ladder, Hannah?"

"I appropriated it from the basement of Dad's hardware store. I figured I might need a ladder so I brought it here when we sold the hardware store."

"You should have appropriated a new aluminum ladder, dear. This one was your Grandpa Swensen's ladder, and I tried for years to get your father to replace it. He finally got a new ladder for the house, but he must have kept this old one for sentimental reasons."

"I can understand that. That's why I wanted to keep it. But I should have propped it up in a corner and bought a new one for us to use. That's what I intended to do, but it slipped my mind."

"I'll remind you," Lisa said quickly. "Don't worry about that!"

"I won't forget again. This is the year we're getting a new one, and I'll order a metal ladder that won't rust. And I'll get one that has actual steps instead of rungs. I'll call to order it right after we hear about Mother's emergency."

"And after we have some coffee and cookies to calm down," Lisa added, turning to Delores. "Let's go to the kitchen. We just finished baking for the day and we made some of Andrea's Red Velvet Whippersnapper Cookies."

Delores smiled. "They sound good. . . . Of course everything you dear girls bake is good." She turned to Hannah. "What are you going to do with that rickety old ladder?"

"I don't know," Hannah admitted as she followed her mother and Lisa into the kitchen. "I'll throw it out, I guess. It's too far gone for anyone to use."

"Don't do that!" Delores objected. "Are you getting your new ladder from Dad's old store?"

"Of course I am. It's the only hardware store in town, and I like Cliff Schumann and his dad."

"Then why don't you ask Cliff to deliver your new ladder and bring the old one to my house?"

"But it's in pieces! Really, Mother . . . I don't think anyone could fix it."

"I won't even try to have it fixed. I just want to keep it around for sentimental reasons."

Hannah stared at her mother in confusion. Delores wasn't usually this sentimental. But if Delores wanted the ladder, Hannah was perfectly willing to give it to her. "Okay. Whatever you want, Mother. I'll call Cliff right now."

"Thank you, dear." Delores took her usual stool at the stainless-steel workstation while Lisa poured coffee and filled a platter with Red Velvet Whippersnapper Cookies from one of the two baker's racks at the side of the kitchen.

Hannah headed for the wall phone in the kitchen, and less than a minute later, she'd ordered the new aluminum ladder for The Cookie Jar and given Cliff instructions to bag up the old wooden ladder and deliver it to her mother's house.

"Okay," she said, sitting down at the workstation and addressing her mother. "Now tell us about your emergency, or whatever it is."

"Just because it may have been down-graded a bit doesn't mean it's not important," Delores maintained.

"Agreed. Tell us, Mother."

Delores sighed. "All right. The emergency, or situation, or whatever it is, is Ricky-Ticky."

"Mayor Bascomb," Lisa said, knowing that Hannah's mother often used the nickname she'd given Mayor Bascomb when he was a small boy and she was his babysitter. "What else has he done?"

"What *else*?" Delores asked, and it was clear that she wasn't sure what Lisa meant.

"Yes, what *else* has he done? Whatever it is, it couldn't be worse than hiring Phyllis Bates and moving her here just because . . . well, you know why he did it. And then, when his wife, Stephanie, got wind of what was going on between the two of them, reassigning Phyllis as Herb's assistant in the town marshal's office!"

Neither Hannah nor Delores knew quite what to say. They'd never seen Lisa quite so angry before. But there was no need to respond because Lisa didn't bother to wait for a reply.

"At least Stephanie Bascomb got her revenge! I saw that diamond ring she made the mayor buy for her and it's as big as a boulder!"

Hannah and Delores exchanged glances. Lisa sounded terribly bitter and they couldn't blame her for that. Lisa's husband, Herb Beeseman, had dated Phyllis Bates in high school and everyone had expected them to get married. But Phyllis's family had moved and Phyllis hadn't bothered to keep in touch with Herb or anyone else in Lake Eden. She hadn't been heard from in several years until Mayor Bascomb had somehow found her. And now she was back in Lake Eden, even more attractive than she'd been in high school.

"Don't keep me in suspense. Tell me what our esteemed mayor did this time," Lisa said, turning to face Delores. "Nothing you say about that man can possibly surprise me!"

"All right, but it's really bad." Delores took another sip of coffee and sat up a little straighter. "I'm warning you, Lisa. . . . This could be even worse than hiring Phyllis in the first place. I got the news this morning, straight from Rod at the *Lake Eden Journal.*" She glanced at her watch. "The paper is coming out in an hour, and I wanted to give you advance warning."

"Advance warning of what?" Lisa asked, looking worried.

"Mayor Bascomb called Rod late last night and said he's not holding the Mrs. Claus contest this year. Instead, he's using his executive authority to appoint someone to play Santa's wife."

Lisa began to look a little sick. "Don't tell me it's . . ." She stopped and swallowed hard.

"I'm afraid it is," Delores answered. "Ricky-Ticky has appointed Phyllis Bates as this year's Mrs. Claus!"

It was all Hannah could do to keep from speaking several words she would never utter around her young nieces. Everyone knew that Lisa had been hoping to be Mrs. Claus this year. Herb had played Santa for the past four years running, passing out gift bags with candy and cookies to the children in the audience right after the Lake Eden Players had performed their Christmas play. Lisa, as Herb's wife in real life, was the logical choice for Mrs. Claus. And everyone, Hannah included, had thought that this would be Lisa's year to have that honor. And now Mayor Bascomb had arbitrarily given the role to Herb's former girlfriend, Phyllis.

Delores reached out to pat Lisa's hand. "To tell the truth, I can't stand Phyllis either. She certainly could never be mistaken for a lady!"

Lisa responded with a shaky smile. "That's true," she said in a small voice.

Hannah wanted to say something supportive, but she wasn't sure what it should be. She didn't like Phyllis either. There had been several incidents in high school involving the bouncy blond cheerleader wearing too-tight sweaters and too-short skirts that had caused Hannah to harbor less than affectionate feelings for her. But telling Lisa about her own feelings wouldn't comfort her. Hannah's great-grandmother Elsa had always said that actions spoke louder than words, and Hannah reached over to give Lisa a hug.

"There's something else I have to tell you," Delores said. "We have to find another candy company. The one the town council used last year just went out of business. That means we can't sell candy during the intermissions. You have no idea how upset Tory is about that! This is her first play and she was hoping it would be a huge success."

"I can understand that," Hannah said. Victoria Bascomb, or Tory, as she preferred to be called, was the mayor's sister. A wealthy and successful actress who had recently retired from the stage, Tory Bascomb had moved to Lake Eden and taken over as the director of the Lake Eden Players.

"We won't have anything to sell at intermission," Delores continued, "not even popcorn now that we lost the popcorn machine."

"*Lost* it?" Hannah was puzzled. How could you lose a concession-stand size popcorn machine? It was huge!"

"Not *that* way! We didn't physically lose it. But we've always borrowed it from Jordan High, and theirs is broken. They're getting a new one, but it won't be here until after Christmas. The Lake Eden Players made a lot of money at the cconcession counter last year. And this year they won't make anything."

"Maybe we can do something about that," Lisa told Delores. "Hannah and I already agreed to make the candy and cookies for the gift bags that Santa will give to the children. There's no reason we can't just double that order."

"But you manned the concession stand last year," Delores pointed out. "Will you have time to do that again and make more candy and cookies, too?"

"We'll make time. It's important to support the Lake Eden Players, and I want to see the play anyway. My mother read *A Christmas Carol* to all of us every year, but

I've never seen the play."

Hannah turned to look at Lisa in shock. Christmas was a very busy season for them. They'd been discussing it over their first cup of coffee this morning, attempting to come up with a schedule that would let them have a little more time off to enjoy the holidays with their friends and families. And now Lisa had volunteered both of them for more work! The play was being performed three times, and the concession stand would be open before the performance, and during the first and second intermissions. They'd have to be there early to set up, wait on customers as they filed in, handle the intermissions, and clean up after the performances.

Why had Lisa done this? For a brief moment Hannah was puzzled, but then she understood the reason why Lisa had taken on this extra work. Now that Phyllis Bates had been cast as this year's Mrs. Claus, Lisa wanted to be there to keep an eye on Herb. Herb and Phyllis would appear on stage together every night after the final curtain had fallen. They'd greet the children who were attending the performance, give them treat bags, and share a hug before they walked off-stage. Lisa wanted to be right there to judge her husband's reaction to that very public hug. But Lisa had never been the jealous type of wife. Why was she so worried about Herb and Phyllis now? Hannah couldn't shake the feeling that there was something else wrong between Herb and Lisa, something that Lisa wasn't telling her.

"Just what we need!" Hannah muttered under her breath, but she managed to maintain her pleasant expression as she turned to her mother. "Do you know how much candy the Lake Eden Players sold at their performance last year?"

"I don't have a dollar amount, but I do know that all our local charities were extremely grateful for their donations."

"Could you get us a copy of last year's order from the candy company?" Lisa asked, clearly realizing why Hannah wanted that information. "We need to know the quantities to be certain that we make enough."

"Of course you need to know the quantity. I should have thought of that. I'll run over to Tory Bascomb's temporary office and ask her." Delores paused to take a bite of her cookie. "And by the way, dears . . . these cookies are fantastic. I love the fact that they have chocolate chips inside."

"I'll tell Andrea you said so," Hannah

promised. "More coffee, Mother?"

"No, dear. I really must go." Delores got up from her stool. "I have a million things to do today. Have fun baking, dears. And be sure to save samples of any new cookies you try. I love to test new cookies for you."

Hannah waited until the back kitchen door had closed behind her mother, and then she turned to Lisa. "Okay, Lisa . . . give!"

"Give what?"

"There's more to this Herb and Phyllis thing than you're telling me."

"You're imagining things," Lisa said, but she looked down at the worktable, not meeting Hannah's eyes.

"I don't think so. And it'll probably help to talk about it. Tell me what's wrong, Lisa."

Lisa sat there in silence for a moment, and then she gave a deep sigh. "Herb's been working late every single night this month. I know he loves me and I know that I should trust him, but it's *every* night."

"When did this start?"

"A couple days after Mayor Bascomb transferred Phyllis to Herb's office."

It was Hannah's turn to sigh. "Did you drive past Herb's office to see if he was there?"

"Yes, after it happened five nights in a row.

And Hannah . . . Herb wasn't there!"

"Maybe he was out on patrol?"

"No. His cruiser was in the lot, right where he always parks it. But his personal car was gone!"

That didn't sound good, and Hannah reached out to pat Lisa's shoulder. "Did you try to find him?"

"Yes. I drove past Dad's house because I thought he might have gone over there to help his mother with something. He wasn't there, and I didn't go in to ask if they'd seen him. I was too embarrassed. I didn't want them to think I was tracking him down!"

"Of course not. Did you try anywhere else?"

"Yes." Lisa gave a little nod. "I drove past every place I could think of, anywhere I thought he might go."

Hannah hated to ask the logical question, but there was no way she could leave that particular stone unturned. "Did you drive past Phyllis Bates's apartment?"

"Yes," Lisa admitted and she looked shamefaced. "I know that a wife should trust her husband, but when I couldn't find Herb anywhere else, I drove out to The Oaks. I didn't want to, but I just had to know!"

"Of course you did," Hannah reassured

her partner, remembering the night she'd driven past the back of the Magnolia Blossom Bakery and spotted Mike's car there. "Was Herb there?"

"No. At least I don't *think* he was there. I didn't spot his car in the visitor parking section."

"How about Phyllis's car?"

"It was in her parking spot. I tried to convince myself that if Phyllis was home and Herb's car wasn't there, he couldn't be with Phyllis. But then I noticed that there were no lights on in her apartment."

"What time was that?"

"A quarter to ten."

"Maybe she was tired and she went to bed early," Hannah suggested, even though she doubted that Lisa would accept that explanation.

"On the *weekend*?" Lisa asked, sounding incredulous. "Phyllis is a party girl. Herb told me that, even back in high school, she'd stay up late and barely make it to school on time the next morning. Their first class was history, and Phyllis slept through it almost every day. Herb had to give her his notes or she would have flunked."

"Herb's right," Hannah conceded. "I sat right across from her and she fell asleep almost every morning. As a matter of fact, she asked me to poke her if she dropped her pen."

They sat in silence for a moment, and then Lisa gave a little shrug. "I can't help but wonder if Herb picked Phyllis up at her place and they went somewhere together. I shouldn't be thinking like that, but maybe Mayor Bascomb isn't the only married man Phyllis has set out to seduce."

RED VELVET WHIPPERSNAPPER COOKIES

DO NOT preheat your oven quite yet — this cookie dough needs to chill before baking.

1 box (**approximately 18 ounces**) red velvet cake mix, the kind that makes a 9-inch by 13-inch cake (**I used Duncan Hines**)

1 large egg, beaten (**just whip it up in a glass with a fork**)

2 cups of Original Cool Whip, thawed (**measure this — a tub of Cool Whip contains a little over 3 cups and that's too much!**)

1 teaspoon vanilla extract

1 cup semi-sweet MINI chocolate chips (**I used Nestle**)

1/2 cup powdered (**confectioner's**) sugar (**you don't have to sift it unless it's got big lumps**)

small jar of red maraschino cherries, cut in half vertically and without stems

Pour HALF of the dry cake mix into a large bowl.

Use a smaller bowl to mix the two cups of Cool Whip with the beaten egg and the vanilla extract. Stir gently with a rubber spatula until everything is combined.

Add the Cool Whip mixture to the cake

mix in the large bowl. STIR VERY CARE-FULLY with a wooden spoon or a rubber spatula. Stir only until everything is combined. You don't want to stir all the air from the Cool Whip.

Sprinkle the rest of the cake mix on top and gently fold it in with the rubber spatula. Again, keep as much air in the batter as possible. Air is what will make your cookies soft and have that melt-in-your-mouth quality.

Sprinkle the cup of semi-sweet mini chips on top and gently fold the chips into the airy cookie mixture. Cover the bowl and chill this mixture for at least one hour in the refrigerator. It's a little too sticky to form into balls without chilling it first.

Hannah's 1st Note: Andrea sometimes mixes whippersnapper dough up before she goes to bed on Friday night and bakes her cookies with Tracey in the morning.

When your cookie dough has chilled and you're ready to bake, preheat your oven to 350 degrees F., and make sure the rack is in the middle position. DO NOT take your chilled cookie dough out of the refrigerator until after your oven has reached the proper temperature.

While your oven is preheating, prepare your cookie sheets by spraying them with

Pam or another nonstick baking spray, or lining them with parchment paper.

Place the confectioner's sugar in a small, shallow bowl. You will be dropping cookie dough into this bowl to form dough balls and coating them with the powdered sugar.

When your oven is ready, take your dough out of the refrigerator. Using a teaspoon from your silverware drawer, drop the dough by rounded teaspoonful into the bowl with the powdered sugar. Roll the dough around with your fingers to form powdered-sugar-coated cookie dough balls.

Hannah's 2nd Note: This is easiest if you coat your fingers with powdered sugar first and then try to form the cookie dough into balls.

Place the coated cookie dough balls on your prepared cookie sheets, no more than 12 cookies on a standard-size sheet.

If you haven't already done so, cut your maraschino cherries in half and place one half, rounded side up, on top of each cookie ball on your baking sheet.

Hannah's 3rd Note: I've said this before, but it bears repeating. Work with only one cookie dough ball at a time. If you drop more than one in the bowl of powdered sugar, they'll stick together.

Andrea's Note: Make only as many cookie dough balls as you can bake at one time and then cover the dough and return it to the refrigerator. I have a double oven so I prepare 2 sheets of cookies at a time.

Bake your Red Velvet Whippersnapper Cookies at 350 degrees F., for 10 to 12 minutes. Test for doneness by tapping them lightly with a finger to see if they're "set."

Let your cookies cool on the cookie sheet for 2 minutes, and then move them to a wire rack to cool completely. (*This is a lot easier if you line your cookie sheets with parchment paper — then you don't need to lift the cookies one by one. All you have to do is grab one end of the parchment paper and pull it, cookies and all, onto the wire rack.*)

Once the cookies are completely cool, store them between sheets of waxed paper in a cool, dry place. (*Your refrigerator is cool, but it's definitely not dry!*)

Yield: 3 to 4 dozen soft, chewy cookies with little nuggets of chocolate inside. Yield will depend on cookie size.

CHAPTER TWO

Lisa wore a slight frown as she got out of Hannah's truck at Jordan High. It was clear that she didn't like what she felt compelled to do. "I feel like I'm spying on Herb by coming here," she confessed as their boots crunched through the freshly fallen snow as they walked toward the entrance of the school auditorium.

"Do you want to forget about it and go home?" Hannah asked her.

"No. I'd just sit there worrying about where Herb was and what he was doing. And thanks to your mother, we do have a perfect excuse for dropping in uninvited."

"That's right." Hannah pulled the heavy door open, and they stepped into the lobby of the auditorium. "We have to pick up the Christmas gift bags from Tory Bascomb. She told Mother she'd leave them on the table in the back of the theater."

Lisa still looked concerned. "Do you think

Herb will think it's strange if we sit down in the back and watch the ending of the play?"

"Absolutely not. He'd be hurt if you told him you were here and you didn't stay to watch his Santa Claus appearance."

"Right," Lisa said, but she didn't sound convinced as she followed Hannah through the inner doors to the auditorium.

The Jordan High auditorium served dual purposes. It was a gymnasium for physical education classes and a basketball court during basketball season. When a theater setting was required, it was a simple matter to pull the velvet curtains partially closed and lower the wall-like curtains that were stored near the ceiling to form a stage at the front center of the court. The unused area at the sides and back served as a large backstage area where the actors could wait for their cues before they appeared onstage. The footlights were cleverly concealed below the floor at the very front, and the stagehands simply released the fasteners that held that section of flooring in place and engaged a lever so the lights swiveled up above the surface of the floor.

Since a rehearsal of the Christmas play was in progress, the basketball court that had been in use the previous night had been turned into a stage setting. The audience area was illuminated only by the lights from the stage, and Lisa and Hannah were quiet as they took seats in the back row to watch the end of the rehearsal.

On the brightly illuminated stage, the Cratchit family was seated around the table for their Christmas feast, and the actor playing Scrooge was with them. Now that Hannah's eyes had adjusted to the lighting, she glanced around the darkened audience area. Counting Lisa and Hannah, there were only six people watching the rehearsal. The director, Tory Bascomb, was seated in the exact center of the audience section, flanked by two nonperforming members of the Lake Eden Players, Irma York and Bonnie Surma, who were acting as her assistants. Immediately in front of Tory was the costume designer, Trudi Schumann. Tory was making notes on a lighted clipboard, and Hannah assumed that she would go over her comments with the cast after rehearsal had concluded.

Bob Cratchit's wife entered, carrying a platter with what was supposed to be a roasted goose, but looked much more like a turkey to Hannah. Mrs. Cratchit set the platter down in the center of the table to a volley of cheers and applause from the diners. Hannah was so busy wondering where the Lake Eden Players' prop master had found a fake turkey that she almost missed the final line of the play. She returned her attention to the stage just in time to hear the boy Tory Bascomb had cast as Tiny Tim, the real son of the actor playing Bob Cratchit, deliver his famous, often-quoted line.

"God bless us, every one," the childish voice rang out loud and clear. There were several long moments of silence onstage while everyone smiled at Tiny Tim, and then Tory Bascomb rose to her feet.

"Curtain!" she yelled. "It's not a tableau, for heaven's sake! Are you back there, Freddy? Or did you decide to take a coffee break?"

"I don't drink coffee, Miss Bascomb!" a male voice, somewhat muffled by the heavy curtains, responded. "Doc says it's not good for me because it makes me too nervous."

"All right then. Listen carefully, Freddy. I've told you this at least a dozen times and I'll skin you alive if you don't get it right on opening night! The instant Tiny Tim delivers his final line, I want you to count to five, and then ring down the curtain."

"I can't, Miss Bascomb."

"Why?"

"Because this curtain doesn't ring. Only

47

bells ring. And this curtain doesn't go down, either. It only goes sideways."

The actor playing Bob Cratchit slapped his hand over his mouth and turned away from the audience. Hannah saw his shoulders shake, and she knew he was laughing. Freddy Sawyer had been born developmentally challenged, but he was a talented handyman and he was willing to work hard. And actually, Freddy did have a point. Tory Bascomb had told him to "ring down" the curtain, and she hadn't explained what that meant.

"Ring down the curtain is a theater phrase, Freddy." Tory did her best to modulate her voice, but she still sounded angry. "All it means is to close the curtains so the audience can't see the actors."

"And the actresses?"

"Yes, and the actresses, too."

"Oh. Okay. I can do that," Freddy said, sounding eager to please the famous actor-director. "I'm sorry I got it wrong, Miss Bascomb."

Irma York, who was acting as one of Tory's assistants, leaned over to whisper something in Tory's ear. Tory nodded, and cleared her throat.

"It's okay, Freddy. Irma's going to come backstage right before the play ends, and she'll tell you when to ring down . . . er . . . never mind. Bonnie will tell you when to close the curtains."

"Gee thanks, Miss Bascomb!" Freddy said, sounding greatly relieved. "I like Irma. She's a friend."

"All right. One more time, people. Let's take it from Mrs. Cratchit's entrance."

Irma climbed the four steps at the side of the auditorium that led up to the stage level and ducked behind the velvet curtains. The actors maintained the places, and the final moments of the play were repeated. Tiny Tim spoke his line, five seconds passed, and then the curtains closed.

"Perfect!" Tory called out. "Good job, Freddy! I'm going to let Irma stay back there and cue you for our Santa and Mrs. Claus appearance. Irma? Can you hear me?"

"Yes, Miss Bascomb."

"We'll open the curtains right after the actors clear and the stagehands dress the set for Santa. Cue Freddy when it's time, will you?"

"Yes, Miss Bascomb," Irma answered, sounding every bit as muffled as Freddy had earlier.

"Sound? Listen up. We'll need the sleigh bells. Make them soft at first and then gradually louder until they reach a peak."

"Got it, Miss Bascomb," someone said from backstage.

"Stagehands?" Tory raised her voice so that the crew could hear her backstage. "I'll need you to move the table to the back of the set just as soon as the actors clear. Then bring in the tree and light it. Set Santa's rocking chair next to the tree."

"Yes, Miss Bascomb," another male voice answered.

"Irma? Just as soon as the stagehands are clear, cue Herb and Phyllis to take their positions in the wings. Then cue Freddy to open the curtains to the dressed, but empty, set."

"Empty, Miss Bascomb?" Irma asked.

"Yes. And the moment the curtains are open fully, the sleigh bells will begin to ring to announce the arrival of Santa and Mrs. Claus. Does everyone have that progression?"

There were murmured assents from behind the curtains, and Tory continued her instructions. "When the sleigh bells reach a peak, Santa and Mrs. Claus will enter stage right. Santa will give us one *'Ho! Ho! Ho!'* and then go directly to his rocker. Once seated, Mrs. Claus will hand him his lap robe and retire to the table, where the Christmas gift bags will be arranged. Is everyone clear on that, so far?"

Again, there were assenting murmurs. Tory waited for a moment and then she called out, "Action!"

Once the curtains opened, Hannah turned to watch Lisa's face in the reflected light from the stage. She looked extremely nervous, and her hands were clasped so tightly in her lap that her knuckles were white.

"Relax. It'll be fine," Hannah whispered, even though she had no valid reason to think that it would be so. Then the sleigh bells began to ring, growing louder and louder, until Santa and Mrs. Claus walked out on the stage.

Hannah heard Lisa's sharp exhalation of breath, and she realized that she had also given a gasp of shock. When she turned to look, Lisa was staring at the stage with an expression of disbelief. Hannah couldn't blame her one bit. Phyllis was wearing a Mrs. Claus costume that was unlike anything Hannah had ever seen before in her life.

The red velvet bodice was so tight, Hannah wondered why she couldn't see the bulge of the fasteners on Phyllis's brassiere. Then she realized that perhaps Phyllis wasn't wearing a brassiere, and she was even more shocked than she'd been before. The red velvet skirt of the costume was short. Very short. And with the display of un-adorned skin with no protection from the winter elements, Mrs. Claus would have been flash frozen like a Popsicle in no time flat.

Santa Claus was wearing heavy winter boots. The height came just under his knees, and the boots matched the ones that had been depicted on countless Christmas cards. Mrs. Claus, on the other hand, was wearing fire-engine-red patent-leather, knee-high boots that perfectly matched the color of her red velvet costume. The heels on the boots were pencil thin, and Phyllis looked erotically alluring. She was a modern, very sexy Mrs. Claus, and no one would ever mistake her for the overweight, jolly, grey-haired Mrs. Claus that smiled continually and baked cookies for Santa's elfin toy-makers.

Hannah turned to look at Lisa, who ap-peared every bit as scandalized as Hannah was. Phyllis Bates wasn't playing Mrs. Claus. She was playing a *Playboy* bunny dressed up as a sexy, over-the-top Mrs. Claus.

Lisa gave an audible gasp as Mrs. Claus bent over to tuck in the lap robe around Santa's knees. Hannah felt like groaning, too. It wasn't her place to do it, but someone had better tell Phyllis never to bend over!

Trudi Schumann turned around to say something to Tory Bascomb. Tory nodded and rose to her feet.

"Mrs. Claus!" Tory called out.

Phyllis stopped arranging the lap robe and turned to face their director. "Yes?"

"Where did you get your costume? And don't try to tell me it was from our costume department, because I know we don't have anything like *that*!"

Phyllis tossed her head, which would normally cause her blond hair to swing in a graceful arc. Now, however, the effect was lost due to the short, curly Mrs. Santa wig she was wearing. "The Mrs. Claus costume you have didn't fit me. I had to go to Minneapolis to get this one."

"Which doesn't fit you, either. It's much too short, much too brief, and much too tight."

"No, this one fits perfectly!" Phyllis argued.

Hannah held her breath. Tory Bascomb had a legendary temper, and Hannah expected it to manifest itself at any moment.

"You're right, Miss Bates. It certainly does fit. It's the perfect costume for a Christmas show in a strip club. But . . . my dear girl . . . *this* is not a strip club. This is general entertainment for men, women, and children of all ages. And there is no way that I will allow you on my stage in a lap dancer's costume!"

Tory turned to Trudi. "Is there any way you can alter our Mrs. Claus costume to fit Miss Bates so that she can return her lamentable and unfortunate choice?"

"Of course, Miss Bascomb. All I need are her measurements and I can have it ready by tomorrow." Even in the darkened theater, Hannah saw that Trudi's lips were twitching with laughter. "I can do it, no problem."

"Then get right on it after tonight's rehearsal. And thank you, Trudi. You've saved us from total disaster." Tory turned to face the stage again. "Now let us put this unfortunate incident behind us and rehearse the rest of the Santa appearance. Miss Bates?"

"Yes?"

Hannah's eyes widened. It was clear that Phyllis was not cowed by the famous director's tone.

"Please go to the table, pick up an imaginary Christmas gift bag, and carry it to Santa."

Hannah and Lisa watched as Phyllis walked to the table, pretended to pick up

54

something from the surface, and returned to hand the nonexistent object to Herb.

"Very good. We'll have a silver tray for the bags the night of the performance. Our prop department tray will hold a dozen bags. All you'll have to do is pick up the tray, stand next to Santa, and hand the bags to him, one by one, after a child is seated on his lap." Tory stopped speaking to smile at Herb. "This year, Trudi has fashioned a new lap robe. Not only is it washable, she has wisely inserted a rubber sheet inside the lining. As our Santa knows quite well, some of the younger children in the audience become a bit too excited when they sit on Santa's lap. This new, improved lap robe should generate a goodly savings for the Lake Eden Players in dry-cleaning costs during the holiday season."

There was a burst of general laughter from backstage, and Hannah glanced at Lisa. Lisa was smiling, and she leaned over to whisper in Hannah's ear.

"They had to dry-clean Herb's costume three times last year. The rubber sheet was my idea."

Tory cleared her throat. "Are you ready, Miss Bates?"

"Ready for what?"

The question from Phyllis was casual, and

Hannah realized that Phyllis was not at all intimidated, even after being dressed down in public by their famous director. Hannah glanced at Lisa, who was frowning slightly, and then she turned back to the stage just in time to watch Tory Bascomb give her next instruction for Herb and Phyllis.

"When the last child leaves, Santa will stand and toss his lap robe on the chair behind him. Action, please, Mr. Beeseman."

Herb got to his feet and tossed the lap robe on the chair.

"Miss Bates? You will stand next to Santa. Santa will put his arms around you and give you a hug."

Hannah wasn't surprised by the instruction. In previous years, Santa had always hugged Mrs. Claus at the end of the show. She watched carefully as Herb put his arms around Phyllis and gave her a hug. Then she glanced at Lisa. Lisa did not look at all upset by the casual hug that Herb had given to Phyllis.

"Perfect," Tory said, cocking her head to the side. "But I think we'll try something new this year. Do you know how to deliver a stage kiss, Miss Bates?"

"I think so. That's a kiss that looks real, but isn't real. Is that right?"

"Basically, yes. This is what I want both of you to do. Mr. Beeseman will pull you into his arms. You, Miss Bates, will reach up to put your hands on his face. Then you will use your thumbs as a barrier and kiss your own thumbs right after Mr. Beeseman turns you to the side so that the audience cannot fully see what you are doing."

"I get it," Phyllis responded quickly.

"Are you sure? Stage-kissing often takes some practice."

Phyllis shook her head. "No, it's okay. I got it."

"All right then. Let's try it. Mr. Beeseman? Please pull Miss Bates into your arms."

As Hannah watched, Herb pulled Phyllis into his arms, but he was careful to keep some space between them. It certainly didn't *look* as if Herb were interested in Phyllis, and that made Hannah doubt that Lisa truly had anything to worry about with her husband. Of course it was always possible that Herb had spotted Lisa in the audience and his apparent disinterest could have been for show. Hannah just wasn't sure.

"Proceed, Miss Bates," Tory directed.

Hannah glanced over at Lisa again. Her hands were clenched in her lap. It was clear that Lisa didn't trust Phyllis to follow the director's instructions.

"Action!" Tory called out, and Phyllis put her hands on Herb's face. Then, without waiting for him to turn, she began to kiss him.

Hannah gave a little gasp. This wasn't a stage kiss. This was real! And Phyllis was kissing Lisa's husband in a *very* passionate way. She reached out for Lisa, wanting to make sure that Lisa stayed in her seat and didn't make a scene right then and there, but her hand encountered empty air. Lisa wasn't there. Her seat was empty. Hannah swiveled around to locate Lisa and spotted her going out the door and into the lobby of the auditorium.

There was only one thing to do. Hannah got up quickly and hurried after Lisa, grabbing the box of Christmas gift bags from the table as she rushed past. The outside door was just closing, and Hannah raced after Lisa, almost slipping on the ice that had gathered on the sidewalk.

"Wait up, Lisa!" she called out, and Lisa stopped under the streetlight that illuminated the parking lot.

There were traces of tears on Lisa's face. Hannah could see them glittering in the light as she approached. Lisa hadn't been fooled for a moment by the stage kiss. And neither had anyone else.

"She kissed him! Like *that*! And she did it right in front of everyone!"

It was useless to deny the truth. Lisa was right. Phyllis had kissed Herb. "I know," Hannah said, reaching out to pat Lisa's shoulder. "But Lisa . . . Herb didn't kiss her. He was expecting a stage kiss. And he wasn't the one who kissed her. Phyllis kissed *him.* Just think about that for a moment. Herb was probably just as shocked as you were. He wasn't expecting it. And there really wasn't anything he could do about it."

"He could have moved. Or he could have pushed her away. He didn't do anything like that! He just stood there."

"Maybe he was too shocked to move or push her away."

"I really doubt that! They were an item in high school. And maybe, just maybe, Herb was enjoying it!"

Hannah remained silent. She knew that there was no way Lisa was going to accept any excuses for Herb right now. She was far too angry. The best thing Hannah could do to defuse the situation was to distract Lisa and give her something else to think about.

"Come on," she said, leading the way to her cookie truck. "Let's take these Christmas gift bags back to The Cookie Jar and see how many pieces of candy they'll hold. We need to figure out how much we need so that we can make out our work schedule. Christmas is a big busy season for us with all the family gatherings and parties."

"You're right," Lisa said, nodding quickly. "We had a lot more dessert-catering jobs than we expected last Christmas."

"That's right. We worked late every night the week before Christmas to fill all those orders."

"And we had to turn down a couple because we just didn't have the time," Lisa recalled. "I'm really sorry, Hannah."

"Sorry for what?" Hannah stopped in the act of buckling her seat belt to ask.

"I'm sorry I volunteered us for even more work by telling your mother we'd make the candy. I should have asked you first."

"Don't be silly. We're partners. I don't ask you every time I accept an order, do I?"

"Well, no. But . . ."

"Then you don't have to ask me," Hannah said before Lisa could go on. "I was just thinking I'd like to try something really different this Christmas."

"What did you have in mind?"

"Something with butterscotch. We've never done anything with butterscotch. I wonder if we could make butterscotch fudge with pretzels in it. Chocolate-covered pretzels are great. Do you think pretzels and butterscotch would go together?"

"I think so. Butterscotch is something almost everyone likes, and you need something salty with the sweetness. If the pretzels don't work, let's see what else we can come up with."

"Okay. We'll experiment."

"Good! I love it when we experiment." Lisa looked excited. "You never know what we're going to come up with, and sometimes it's wonderful!"

"And sometimes it's not," Hannah reminded her.

"I know, but usually something good comes out of it."

"Like, remind me never to try this again because it's yucky?"

Lisa laughed and Hannah breathed a sigh of relief. She'd managed to distract Lisa from her problems.

"Do you have time to do a little experimentation tonight?" Hannah asked her.

"I've got nothing but time. The only thing I have to do tonight is give the dogs their dinner, let them run around the backyard for a while, try my chocolate caramels one more time, and go to bed."

61

"How about Herb? Will he mind if you're late getting home?"

Lisa's expression changed to one mixed between sadness and irritation. "He hasn't been home before midnight for I can't remember how long, and there's no reason to think tonight will be any different."

Hannah was silent. She had no comment. She wished she hadn't asked the question. She wanted to comfort Lisa, to tell her that everything would be okay, but she wasn't sure that would be the case. Was it better to pretend that she wasn't as concerned as Lisa was? She knew that Herb loved Lisa. But sometimes a momentary passion superseded a steady and abiding love. It wasn't right, but it *did* happen and it would be fruitless to deny it. The better choice would be to pick up on something else Lisa had told her. And that was exactly what Hannah did.

"You made chocolate caramels?" Hannah asked, driving out of the snow-covered parking lot behind the school.

"Yes. I tried my great-aunt's recipe last night. It worked, but I want to try it one more time to make sure. Then I'll bring some for you to taste. I sent a dozen to work with Herb this morning, and he called me at The Cookie Jar to say he really liked them. He said he gave one to Phyllis and she wanted another, but he told her he was saving them for later." Lisa gave a little smile. "At least she didn't get *everything* she wanted from him!"

"Right." Hannah decided that the safest thing to do was to change the subject. "If your caramels work out tonight, we can make some for the Christmas gift bags. I don't know anybody who doesn't like caramels."

"Neither do I," Lisa concurred. "But I shouldn't have mentioned them, Hannah."

"Why not?"

Lisa gave a little laugh. "Because now I'm getting hungry. And I don't think there's much in the refrigerator at home except the bologna and cheese for Herb's favorite sandwiches in the morning."

"Now that you mention it, I'm getting hungry, too," Hannah admitted. Then she thought back to her schedule for the day and gave a wry smile. "No wonder! I was so busy, I forgot to eat lunch."

"Me, too. We had a big lunch crowd today and I didn't even think of it. I guess I could have had a couple of cookies, but what I really wanted was meat."

"I know that feeling." Hannah drove down the alley and turned into the parking lot behind The Cookie Jar. "All I can think about is a double cheeseburger with crispy fries."

"And maybe a salad with bleu cheese dressing and some cheesy garlic bread?"

"Oh, yes!" Hannah's mouth began to salivate, and she swallowed. "I've got a proposition for you, Lisa."

"What's that?"

"Let's figure out how much candy the bags will hold and draw up a schedule of what to make when. And after we're through, we can go out to the Corner Tavern for salads, garlic bread, cheeseburgers, and fries."

"And maybe some of their Chocolate Coffee Cake for dessert?"

"Why not!"

Lisa began to smile from ear to ear. "That sounds really good to me, Hannah!"

As Hannah parked, Lisa grabbed the box with the Christmas gift bags for the children, and then she opened the passenger door.

"You're in a hurry?" Hannah asked.

"Yes! Come on, Hannah. I'm so hungry, my stomach is growling just thinking about the fries and onion rings at the Corner Tavern. And the sooner we get started, the sooner we can drive out there and eat!"

CHAPTER THREE

The bar at the Corner Tavern was crowded, but Hannah found a spot near one end. She ordered a soda water with a wedge of lime and sat there waiting for Lisa to arrive. Lisa had stopped at home to feed her dogs, Dillon and Sammy, and let them out to run in the backyard for a few minutes. Hannah had driven out ahead of her to wait for a table for the two of them in the dining room.

The scent of good beef was in the air, and Hannah smiled as she thought of a hot, fresh cheeseburger and crispy golden French fries. The Corner Tavern was a mecca for hamburger and steak lovers. As a nod to their patrons who were cutting down on red meat, they had a vegetarian entrée on their menu, and several fish dishes. The owner's wife, Nona Prentiss, had told Hannah that only two out of a hundred customers ordered a non-beef entrée, and Hannah believed it. As far as she was concerned, the

Corner Tavern had the best beef of any restaurant in the area, perhaps even in the whole state of Minnesota. The reason most people went out there to eat was to get succulent beef, expertly cooked, and plenty of it.

"So, Hannah! How's it going?" a voice called out, and Hannah spotted Bonnie Surma sitting at the bar.

"Everything's fine, Bonnie," Hannah responded. Just then, the man next to Hannah got up to follow one of the waitresses to a table, and Bonnie moved over to sit down on the stool the man had just vacated.

"Can I buy the best baker in Lake Eden a drink?" Bonnie asked, smiling at Hannah.

"Thanks, but I'm just having soda water. Are you meeting someone, Bonnie?"

"Yes, Trudi Schumann. We're going to get a table in the back, as far away from the actors as we can get."

Hannah thought fast. There was only one group of actors in Lake Eden. "Are you talking about the Lake Eden Players?"

"Yes. And Tory Bascomb. She's got the big table in the middle of the room, and she's holding a meeting with the cast."

"And you're not invited?"

"I'm part of the technical crew on the Christmas play. I don't have to go to the actors' meetings, thank goodness. Tory's probably picking apart everyone's performances."

"You don't like Tory?"

Bonnie shrugged. "I like her well enough, but she's very exacting. We're not professionals, and our actors aren't really used to that. The only reason I'm here is that I'm waiting for Trudi. I told her I'd help her alter that Mrs. Santa Claus outfit for Phyllis Bates if she'd come out here for a cheeseburger and a pitcher of beer with me. I'm husband-less tonight. Gil's gone, and I hate to eat alone."

"Is Gil busy with school things?"

"He's in St. Cloud with the chess team. They drove up this afternoon and they're staying overnight. The boys have a competition tomorrow, and they won't be home until late tomorrow night."

Bonnie took a sip from her beer glass, and Hannah noticed that her hands were shaking. "Are you cold, Bonnie?"

"I'm freezing. I had to park all the way in the back, and the wind felt like needles of ice when I got out of the car." She glanced down at her beer glass. "I should have ordered a coffee drink. It's just that I know we'll have beer when Trudi gets here, and I didn't want to mix my drinks. They have

Beck's on tap, and Trudi likes Beck's."

"Why don't you order a cup of coffee on the side? That way you can have your beer and warm up, too."

"Good idea." Bonnie crooked her finger at the bartender, and he came over. "Could I have coffee? I'm still really cold."

"No problem. It's on the house." The bartender poured a cup of coffee and set it in front of Bonnie. "Do you want some brandy in that?"

"No, thanks. I'm meeting someone in a while and we'll be drinking beer." Bonnie turned back to Hannah when the bartender had left. "Are you waiting for someone, Hannah?"

"Yes, Lisa. She had to go home and feed the dogs."

"I saw her in the audience at the rehearsal tonight." Bonnie cupped her hands around the coffee cup to warm them. "Was she terribly upset about that stage kiss that wasn't a stage kiss?"

"Let's just say that she wasn't exactly happy about it."

"I don't blame her for that. And she wasn't the only one who was upset! I saw Herb afterward, and he looked really embarrassed."

"Does Herb know that Lisa was in the

audience?"

"I don't know. I didn't mention it, that's for sure. I figured the less said, the better."

"How about Herb? Is he here at Tory's meeting?"

"I don't know. He hasn't come in since I've been here, but I didn't come straight out. I stopped at the community center to drop off some books I collected for the library. And then I ran past the house to store some things that came for the school."

"Are you still filling in as the librarian when Marge can't make it?"

"Yes, I tried to get out of it this year, but they couldn't find anyone else. I'd like to back off a bit, but I guess I just can't say no, especially if something is school related. Gil doesn't like me to work, but he's okay if I do volunteer things. And I really do enjoy working with the students. And of course I love the Lake Eden Players. I've been working with them for years now."

Hannah was still thinking of that table in the center of the room and exactly who was attending Tory Bascomb's meeting. "Speaking of the Lake Eden Players, do you know if Phyllis Bates is here?"

"She hasn't come in since I've been here. If you want to pop in to look, I'll hold your stool for you."

"Thanks, Bonnie." Hannah got up from her stool and walked over to the entrance to the dining room. The Lake Eden Players weren't difficult to spot since Bonnie had told her that they had the big oval table in the center of the room. Hannah scanned all sides of the table. Herb wasn't there, and neither was Phyllis. She breathed a sigh of relief as she turned to walk back to the bar. If either Herb or Phyllis had been at the table, she would have called Lisa on her cell phone, made some excuse about how the Corner Tavern was too crowded to get a table, and suggested that they meet at Bertanelli's for a pizza instead. As it turned out, Hannah barely had time to finish her soda water before Lisa came in.

"It's a madhouse out there," Lisa said. "I'm just lucky I got here when I did." She noticed Bonnie on the stool next to Hannah and gave a little wave. "Hi, Bonnie."

"Hi, Lisa. What's wrong out there? Are people driving badly?" Bonnie asked, moving over one stool so that Lisa could sit next to Hannah.

Lisa shook her head. "No, it's not that. The drive out was fine, but everyone must have decided to come out here for a hamburger at the same time tonight. There were four cars behind me when I pulled into the parking lot, and I got the last empty spot."

Lisa slid onto the stool and ordered a hot lemonade. It had just arrived when the waitress tapped Hannah on the shoulder to say that their table was ready.

"Do you want to sit with us, Bonnie?" Hannah asked.

"Thanks for the offer, but Trudi should be here any minute now. I'll just stay here and wait for her. I don't want to go in the dining room quite yet. Tory is still holding court with the actors."

Lisa waited until they got to the doorway to the dining room, and then she leaned close to Hannah. "Is Herb here?"

"No."

"Good! At least I think it's good. How about Phyllis?"

"No." Hannah saw the expression on Lisa's face and hurried to reassure her. "But just because neither one of them is here doesn't mean that they're together."

"True. And I'm too hungry to worry about it right now." Lisa took a seat at the table the waitress had indicated and picked up the menu. "I don't really need this. I know exactly what I want. I've been thinking about it for almost an hour now."

Their waitress had carried in their drinks from the bar and she set them on cocktail napkins. "How do you like our new napkins?"

Hannah lifted her drink and saw that the napkin had a picture of a bear on it. "Is that Albert?" she asked, referring to the stuffed grizzly bear that guarded the entrance to the dining room.

"Yes, it's Albert. The boss hired a photographer to take the picture and had the napkins printed. Everybody loves Albert." The waitress pulled an order book from her apron pocket and turned to Lisa. "I can take your order right now, if you want."

"I want." Lisa gave a little laugh. "I'll have a double cheeseburger with a side order of onion rings and three pickles."

"Mustard or ketchup for your burger?"

"Both, please. And a bowl of bleu cheese dressing."

"You want a small green salad, too?" the waitress asked Lisa.

"No. I just like to dip my onion rings in the dressing." Lisa grinned at Hannah. "I got it from her. That's what Hannah does with her French fries."

"It sounds good. I'll have to try it sometime." The waitress turned to Hannah. "And what can I get for you?"

"Exactly the same thing, but I want French fries instead of onion rings. And just put a little extra dressing in that bowl for me."

The waitress laughed. "You can have your own bowl of dressing. It's not like I wash the dishes around here."

Hannah waited until their waitress had left, and then she leaned forward. "Well? Did you do it?"

"Do what?"

"You know what I mean."

Lisa nodded. "Yes. I didn't want to, but I couldn't help it."

"I figured you would. And we *are* talking about the same thing, aren't we?"

Lisa laughed. "I think so. You wanted to know if I drove past her apartment . . . right?"

"Right. Did you learn anything?"

"Only that her apartment was dark and her car was gone."

"How about Herb's office?"

"The lights were off, his cruiser was in the lot, and Herb's car wasn't there." Lisa reached for the small bowl of pickled vegetables that was sitting on their table. "I love these pickles."

"Me, too."

Hannah thought about the custom that the Corner Tavern had followed since their opening day. After the busboy cleared a table and reset it for the next diners, he dished up a small bowl of pickled vegetables and put it in the center of the table. It was a fresh bowl every time and, in the beginning, the original owner's wife, Nona's predecessor, had pickled all the vegetables herself.

"I love this pickled cauliflower," Lisa said, crunching down on the vegetarian treat.

"And I love these." Hannah reached for a green string bean and bit off half. "Did you know that my great-grandmother used to call pickled vegetables *digestives*?"

"No. Are digestives something that helps you digest food?"

"Supposedly. Of course in the United Kingdom, they have digestive biscuits to take care of that. The first digestives were a sweet meal biscuit. They were meant to get the digestive juices flowing and make it easier for the body to process the rest of the meal."

"Believe me, my digestive juices are flowing!" Lisa smacked her lips. "These are really good. Can I have the last piece of cauliflower?"

"Knock yourself out. I'm enjoying the green beans and the button mushrooms."

For a few more moments the conversation consisted solely of crunching and chewing. Then Lisa looked down at the empty bowl.

"Good heavens! We even ate the pickled carrots. And I don't like the pickled carrots!"

Their waitress overheard Lisa's comment and came over to take the empty bowl. "You two must really be hungry. I've been working here for over ten years and I've never seen an empty relish bowl. Nobody ever eats the carrots."

"Then why are they there?" Lisa asked her.

"Search me!"

"They're probably for color," Hannah offered an explanation. "Without them, the bowl would consist of green, white, and tan. That's not as eye-catching as a mixture with orange in it."

"You've got a point there," the waitress complimented Hannah. "Too bad they don't pickle those little red cherry tomatoes. They'd be really pretty."

Hannah thought about that for a moment. "You're right. And I wonder if you could pickle them. I think I'll give it a try."

"They'd be good in salads, too," the waitress said.

"And you could use them to decorate a bowl of coleslaw, or potato salad," Lisa suggested.

The waitress reached into her pocket and pulled out an electronic device. "Your food's up," she told them once she'd glanced at the display. "I'll go get it, and then you can eat something besides pickles."

"I'm positively stuffed!" Lisa remarked, as they got into their parkas and put on gloves and hats.

"Me, too. Maybe we shouldn't have had that Chocolate Coffee Cake for dessert."

"Or maybe we shouldn't have split that second order of French fries," Lisa added.

For once, the wind wasn't blowing as they went out the door, and the night was clear and icy cold. Both Hannah and Lisa shivered as they walked into the parking lot.

"Where did you park, Hannah?"

"I'm way in the back of the lot by the ditch."

"I'm back there, too. Let's walk over on the side, where there's fresh snow. It's not as slippery there."

The walking was easier once they'd moved to the side of the lot and they could avoid the deep ruts that the cars had made driving in and out. Hannah and Lisa had arrived at the back row when Hannah spotted something at the edge of the ditch.

"Wait up a second, Lisa," Hannah said. "Someone dropped something red in the snow and I want to see what it is."

"I see it. It looks like cloth."

"It's probably nothing but a mitten or a scarf, but whoever lost it might want it back."

"I can go with you."

"Better not. It's outside the plowed area and the snow's deep out there. It could go right over your ankle boots."

Hannah waded into the area that hadn't been plowed, heading straight toward the red object. As she got closer, she could see that Lisa had been right. It was something made of red cloth.

"It's a Santa hat!" Hannah called out to Lisa. "And there's something else here, too. Hold on and I'll see what it is."

As she waded even farther into the ditch, Hannah began to feel increasingly anxious. The anxious, uneasy feeling had nothing to do with the cold or the snow. There was something wrong, very wrong.

Hannah's first instinct was to turn around and retrace her steps up the side of the ditch and into the bright lights and safe haven of the parking lot. But she couldn't seem to turn around without knowing what had given her that anxious, uneasy feeling, and her need to know pulled her even deeper into the ditch.

The moon cast a cold, blue light over the

surface of the snow. There were icicles with their sharp, lethal points hanging from the stark black branches of the trees. Hannah shuddered. She'd always felt menaced whenever she had to pass under icicles, but the trees with their glittering daggers dotted the sides of the ditch. There was no other path she could take to get to the second object she'd seen.

As she neared the bottom of the ditch, her heart was racing and Hannah was breathing in painful gasps. This wasn't from the exertion of wading through deep snow. It was fear of something she had yet to discover.

Her boot hit something beneath the snow, and Hannah barely managed to maintain her balance. She reached down to uncover the object that had tripped her, and her gloved fingers drew it out of the snow. She stood there staring for a moment, puzzled by the sight of one of the reusable lunch bags that Lisa had given to Herb for Christmas. Each lunch bag was a different color, and they all had Herb's name embroidered on the side in bold black letters.

There was something inside the bag, and Hannah made sure the contents didn't fall out as she flipped it over so that she could see the other side. A chill ran through her. The lunch bag was definitely Herb's. She could read his name quite clearly in the cold, blue moonlight. But why was Herb's lunch bag buried in the snow near the bottom of the ditch?

A possible explanation occurred to Hannah. Herb could have disliked the lunch that Lisa had packed for him and, quite literally, ditched it before he'd gone inside to eat lunch. This was possible, but very unlikely. Herb told everyone who would listen about the wonderful lunches his wife made for him and how much he enjoyed them. And even if he hadn't felt like eating this particular day's lunch and had thrown it out, Herb would have kept the lunch bag to take home to Lisa.

Her curiosity aroused, Hannah opened the lunch bag and peeked inside. There was no sandwich, or fruit, or cookies. The only thing left in the bag was homemade candy wrapped in waxed paper. Lisa's caramels. And Herb had told Lisa that he loved them. Why had he eaten part of his lunch and then thrown away his personalized lunch bag containing Lisa's caramels?

Hannah's mind was working on this new puzzle when she spotted something else only a few feet away. As she stared at the bulky, snow-covered mound, the anxious, uneasy feeling in her stomach began to intensify. She thrust the lunch bag in the pocket of her parka. She'd dispose of it later. There was no way she was going to let Lisa see what had happened to her caramels. Lisa would be devastated by the fact that Herb had lied to her by saying he liked her caramels and then throwing them away.

As Hannah stepped toward the mound in the snow, she had a very unwelcome thought. It was human-sized. "No!" she gasped as an awful suspicion took root in her mind. "It can't be!" she exclaimed, aloud.

"Hannah? Are you all right?" Lisa's voice floated down to her from above.

"I'm okay. I'm just . . ." Hannah thought fast. There was no way she was going to alarm Lisa before she found out what was in that mound of snow. "I'm just winded and I have to catch my breath. The snow is really deep down here."

Hannah was amazed at how strong and steady her voice was. Perhaps she should join the Lake Eden Players. It seemed as if she could act, since she felt just the opposite of strong and steady. "I'm just going to check out one more thing while I'm down here, and then I'll climb back up."

As she approached the hump of snow, Hannah realized that the anxious feeling in her stomach was what Mike had called her *slaydar,* her uncanny penchant for finding murder victims. *Please let it be wrong this time,* Hannah's mind begged, but that sick, sinking feeling grew with each step she took toward the snow-covered mound.

"Please not Herb!" she whispered as she brushed off a layer of snow with her gloves. She swept another layer to the side, and then another, until she had uncovered a cold, dead body that made her give an audible gasp of shock.

"What did you find, Hannah?" Lisa called out from the top of the ditch.

Hannah swallowed hard, and somehow she managed to form the words she needed to say. "Call Mike!"

"Mike? You mean . . . oh, no!"

"Yes!" Hannah answered, and then she swallowed again. "Tell him to get out here right away!"

"I will. Right now. Are you all right?"

"Yes. Hurry, Lisa. Tell him I'll stay where I am until he gets here."

Hannah listened as Lisa made the call. Her words were succinct and she sounded in control. Hannah was very grateful that Lisa had pulled herself together. The ditch was deep, and even though she had her cell phone with her, she might not have been able to get reception down there.

"He said to hang on, he'll be right there. Who . . ." Lisa stopped in mid-question and gave a little sob. "Who is it, Hannah?"

"Phyllis. Phyllis Bates."

"Is she . . . uh . . . is she . . . dead?"

Hannah glanced down at the cold, motionless body that had been very alive in a sexy Mrs. Santa costume not even two hours ago. Her eyes swept up to the damage that had been done to Phyllis's head, and she swallowed hard again. "Yes, Lisa. Phyllis is dead."

CHAPTER FOUR

When Hannah unlocked the door to her condo, she stepped back three paces and braced herself. Then she leaned forward, pushed open the door, and waited for the feline missile that was about to launch itself in her direction. She waited . . . and waited . . . and then the orange-and-white missile hurtled into her arms.

"Moishe! Where were you?" Hannah asked, carrying her cat in to place him in his favorite spot on the top of the couch.

"Sorry," her sister Michelle said, rushing out of the guest bedroom. "I was just showing Moishe his new cat toy, and we didn't hear you unlock the door."

"Michelle!" Hannah greeted her youngest sister with a big hug. "How did you get here?"

Michelle laughed. "If you'd checked your text messages, you'd know. Mother picked me up at the bus station and dropped me off here two hours ago. I hope you don't mind that I used the key you gave me and came inside."

"Why should I mind? That's why I gave you that key in the first place." Hannah knew she probably looked a little crazy, but she couldn't seem to stop smiling. Seeing Michelle making herself at home in the condo was like basking in the sunshine. "I'm so glad you're here!"

"Uh-oh, this sounds like trouble!" Michelle said, hurrying to the kitchen to take the glass of white wine she'd poured in preparation for Hannah's return from the top shelf in the refrigerator. "Sit down, kick off your boots, and tell me all about it."

Hannah peeled off her parka, kicked off her boots on the rug by the door, and took a seat on her old couch. "Just for starters, Phyllis Bates is dead."

"Mayor Bascomb's new squeeze?"

Hannah nodded. "That's right. I found her in the ditch behind the Corner Tavern parking lot."

"Murdered?"

"Oh, yes. As far as I know, people don't usually bash in their own heads as a pre-ferred method of suicide."

It was clear that Michelle was attempting to control herself, but it didn't work. She laughed. "That's what I love about you, Hannah. You don't mince words."

"Well . . . perhaps that was a bit insensitive, but it's true."

"Yes, it's insensitive, but it was funny. And you found her?"

"Who else?" Hannah removed the plastic wrap from the top of the wineglass and took a sip. "I have slaydar, remember?"

"How could I forget? Mike says that all the time. Is he coming over tonight to take your statement?"

"That's what he said. Do I have any food in the house?"

"You do now. I brought some groceries with me on the bus, and I can make supper. The only thing I forgot was the Thousand Island dressing, but I guess I could get along without it."

"You don't have to get along without it."

Michelle smiled. "Great! Do you have some in the refrigerator?"

"No, but I have everything you need to make it. All it is is mayonnaise mixed with ketchup and sweet pickle relish."

"How much?"

"Just mix it to taste. It'll be exactly the same as the bottled dressing. What are you planning to make?"

"Grilled Ham and Double Cheese Sandwiches."

"That sounds like a really good sandwich!"

"It is. I made them for my housemates last night, and they said they loved them."

Hannah smiled. "I'm sure they did. You're a good cook, Michelle."

"Thanks. I'll make two for Mike and one for me. Do you want me to make one for you?"

"I'd love to try one, but I already ate a double cheeseburger, an order and a half of fries with bleu cheese dressing, and a slice of Chocolate Coffee Cake."

"Will you at least taste a corner of mine?"

"Of course I will. What kind of bread do you use?"

"Rye. There's a bakery near us, and they make really good breads."

"It sounds wonderful, and I almost wish I hadn't eaten. But I was *really* hungry."

"It only takes a few minutes to make them, so I won't start until Mike gets here. I'm experimenting with quick meals. One of my roommates is getting married right after graduation, and I want to give her a whole folder of easy, quick suppers. Her boyfriend's a teacher, and that's what she'll be when she graduates."

"That sounds like a great wedding gift,

Michelle."

Michelle looked pleased. "I thought it would be better than monogrammed sheets or a set of fancy towels she'd only get out when company was coming."

After Michelle had gone into the kitchen, Hannah changed to her favorite wintertime at-home outfit which consisted of forest-green sweatpants, an oversized sweatshirt of the same color, and fur-lined slippers. Then she sat down on the couch again, picked up her wineglass, and took another sip. The Cookie Jar was doing good business, she'd finished her Christmas shopping early this year, and Michelle was in town. Life in Lake Eden was very good if you didn't consider the murder rate.

The knock on the door came twenty minutes later, and Michelle got up to answer it. "Good thing I decided to put together a double batch," she said as she saw that Lonnie was with Mike.

"A double batch of what?" Mike asked, sniffing the air as he walked into the living room. "Whatever it is, it smells great!"

"Michelle baked cookies earlier," Hannah told him, getting up to greet them, "and she's making Grilled Ham and Double Cheese Sandwiches." She turned to smile at

Lonnie. "Hi, Lonnie. I guess you two guys are working late tonight."

"We're waiting for Doc to finish the autopsy," Mike explained. "And I have to complete your statement. After that, we're through."

"Except for being on call," Lonnie added. "We're on call twenty-four-seven during homicide investigations."

"Do you want to interview Hannah now?" Michelle asked Mike. "Or would you rather wait until after you eat?"

"Now. I've got most of what I need, and it shouldn't take more than ten minutes." Mike walked over to the couch, sat down, and patted the cushion next to him. "Come over here, Hannah. Lonnie can keep Michelle company in the kitchen."

Hannah took a seat on the cushion next to Mike. "What else do you need to know?"

"I need answers to a couple of questions that occurred to me after you'd left. Did you see the body from the top of the ditch?"

"No. The ditch is quite deep, and it was too dark to see much of anything. I just happened to notice something red in the snow, and I went to see what it was."

"Did you think it was blood?"

"No, not at all. Both Lisa and I could see that it was something made of cloth. I

88

thought it was a mitten, or a glove, or maybe a scarf. And since it wasn't that far from the lip of the ditch, I told Lisa that I was going to climb down to get it."

"You told me that earlier, but you didn't tell me why."

For a moment, Hannah was puzzled. "Why what?"

"Why did you go down to get it?"

"Oh. Because somebody had obviously lost whatever it was and I thought they might have wanted it back."

Mike smiled at her. "That figures. You're just a helpful person by nature. Why didn't Lisa go with you?"

"She would have, but the snow was deep and she was wearing ankle boots. I had my regular boots on and they're knee-highs. It was a good thing, too. The snow was really deep down there."

"And the cloth you spotted was . . . ?"

"A Santa hat. I picked it up and I intended to climb right back up when I saw something else."

"The body?"

"Actually . . . no. I hadn't seen that yet. It was at the bottom of the ditch. I thought I'd spotted something else, but I couldn't find it again when I got down there. But I did find something else quite near the bottom."

"What was that?"

"I'll tell you, but it's something very . . ." Hannah paused, searching for the right word. "Let's just say that it was something very sensitive."

"Something sensitive in what way?"

"Well . . ." Hannah paused again and took a moment to formulate her answer. "Look, Mike . . . do you really have to put what I tell you in your report?"

"That depends on whether or not it has anything to do with the investigation."

"But if it's just personal and it doesn't have anything to do with the murder, then you don't have to put it in your report, do you?"

"I'll have to make up my own mind on that, Hannah. And I'll do that *after* you tell me what it was."

Hannah sighed deeply. She wished she'd never mentioned that second object, but she had and now she was obligated to tell Mike.

"Hannah?"

"Yes. I know. I have to tell you. But first, I have to know if you really like Lisa."

Mike reared back in surprise. "Of course I like Lisa! She's like a younger sister to me."

"Okay. How about Herb? Do you like Herb?"

The puzzled expression on Mike's face didn't change with this new question. "Sure, I do. Herb's a regular guy. What's this all about, Hannah?"

"It's complicated." Hannah took a moment to phrase her answer. "Lisa's worried that Herb was getting a little too close and personal with Phyllis Bates, now that Mayor Bascomb reassigned her to Herb's office. Herb's been coming home really late almost every night, and Lisa knows he's not at work because she drove past his office and his car wasn't there."

"Okay. As far as I know, Herb's crazy about Lisa and I don't believe he'd get involved with another woman, but go on."

"Lisa made chocolate caramels last night and gave some to Herb in his lunch bag."

"That's nice, but what does that have to do with Phyllis Bates?"

"I'll tell you, but please be careful with this. If it gets out, it could cause a lot of trouble between Lisa and Herb."

"Okay. That's enough salad. Let's get to the main course. Spit it out, Hannah."

"The object I found was Herb's lunch bag. It was one of the reusable, personalized ones that Lisa gave him as a present.

91

The lunch was gone, but the caramels were still there. I'm hoping that Herb was saving them for later, Phyllis grabbed Herb's lunch bag after he left the office, and Herb had nothing to do with the fact that she had it with her when she was killed."

"So you want me to sit on that piece of information until I find out if Herb has an alibi?"

Hannah nodded gratefully. "Yes, that's it exactly. Please, Mike . . . I just can't believe that Herb could kill anyone."

"Of course you can't, but both of us know that the most unlikely people can kill if they believe the circumstances warrant it."

"I know you're right, but I still can't believe it."

Mike reached out to slip an arm around Hannah's shoulders. "Okay. Just think about this for a minute. Say Herb *is* having a fling with Phyllis and Phyllis is threatening to tell Lisa about it unless he does something for her. And whatever that something is, Herb can't do it. He doesn't want to lose Lisa. He loves her. But Herb knows that Phyllis is the type of woman to make good on her threat and wreck his marriage. Herb's caught in a vise, and it's getting tighter with each passing day. He's desperate and he can see only one way out of it. He has to neutralize the threat."

Hannah shivered and Mike pulled her a bit closer. "By killing Phyllis before she can talk to Lisa?"

"Yes. You said that Lisa was with you when you found the body. Do you know where she was *before* she met you at the Corner Tavern?"

"Yes. You know that Herb's playing Santa and Mayor Bascomb appointed Phyllis as Mrs. Claus, don't you?" Mike nodded, and Hannah continued. "Lisa and I went to the rehearsal to pick up the Christmas gift bags we're filling with candy for the children. We sat down in the back of the auditorium and watched the last few minutes of the play. And then it was time for Herb and Phyllis to come onstage."

"Lisa wanted to watch Herb with Phyllis?"

Hannah nodded. "And that turned out to be a really bad idea. Tory Bascomb directed Phyllis to give Herb a stage kiss right before the final curtain, but Phyllis really kissed him. I mean, *really* kissed him. It was obvious to everyone who saw it that there was nothing staged about that kiss!"

"Go on."

"Lisa and I were sitting in the back, and we saw what everyone else saw. Naturally,

Lisa was upset and she ran out of the auditorium. I caught her on the way to the parking lot, and since I didn't want her to go straight home when she was that upset, we went back to The Cookie Jar and we worked for a while. Then I suggested hamburgers at the Corner Tavern, and Lisa agreed. She said she had to go home to feed the dogs and let them out in the yard for a while before she could go out to eat, but she promised to meet me at the Corner Tavern just as soon as she could."

"Do you know what time you and Lisa left The Cookie Jar?"

"Yes. I looked at the clock before we went out the door. It was only a couple of minutes after nine."

"And what time did Lisa get to the Corner Tavern?"

"I don't remember. I went out there right away and sat at the bar for a while, waiting for a table in the dining room. I didn't look at my watch when Lisa got there, but Bonnie Surma was sitting next to me and she might remember."

"Okay. Give me your best estimate."

"Maybe ten o'clock or a little before that. I know we didn't leave the Corner Tavern until eleven. The receipt was time-stamped."

"Do you still have the receipt?"

"Yes. It's in my purse. I'll get it for you. But I don't understand why you need . . ." Hannah stopped in mid-sentence as the full implication of Mike's questioning hit her. "Do you think that Lisa killed Phyllis?"

"Anything's possible when jealousy is a motive. But no, I don't think that Lisa killed her. I just know that I have to clear her, especially because her car was parked in the back row of the parking lot and that's about where Phyllis would have tumbled down the ditch."

"The sandwiches are ready!" Michelle called out from the kitchen. "Are you ready to eat, Mike?"

"I'm ready," Mike said, giving Hannah a little hug before he stood up to go to the table. "Don't worry, Hannah. I'll get to the bottom of this."

Hannah went to the table, tasted a corner of Michelle's sandwich, and pronounced it excellent. Then she sat there while the others ate and the conversation flowed around her. She made a comment once in a while, just so that no one would notice that she was preoccupied, and she gave a sigh of relief when the evening was over and Michelle went to bed.

Once the condo was silent, Hannah sat on the couch in the darkness with Moishe purring on her lap. She thought about everything that had happened during the day. Yes, even though it was unlikely, it was possible that Herb had killed Phyllis. And even though she felt like a traitor for admitting it, it was also possible that Lisa's temper had flared when she'd seen Phyllis in the parking lot, and she'd struck out with whatever hard object had been at hand.

Hannah shivered and bent over to hug Moishe. His purr was comforting, and she was glad he was keeping her company tonight. Phyllis had craved being the center of attention. She had gloried in causing trouble because it made her feel sexy and powerful. This time, Phyllis had caused trouble for two of Hannah's best friends, her partner, Lisa, and her former high school classmate, Herb. What Phyllis had done was far-reaching. It might have wrecked Lisa and Herb's marriage, and that made Hannah angry and sad at the same time. Perhaps it was a lucky thing that Phyllis wasn't here, sitting next to Hannah on the couch right now.

What Mike had said tonight was true. Anyone was capable of murder under the right circumstances. Even Hannah Swensen.

GRILLED HAM AND DOUBLE CHEESE SANDWICHES

For each sandwich you will need:

2 slices of bread (**Michelle used seedless rye. You could use any kind of bread you prefer.**)

softened butter to spread on the outside of the bread and to put in the frying pan or grill if needed

Thousand Island dressing

1 slice of American cheese

1 fairly thick slice of fully cooked ham

1 slice of Swiss cheese

thin slices of sweet pickles, dill pickles, or sweet onion (**optional**)

Butter two slices of bread. Place one slice, buttered side down, on a piece of wax paper. Spread the bread with a thin layer of Thousand Island dressing. This layer of dressing should not be too thick or your sandwich will get too "gloppy" when you fry it. (**Feel free to add "gloppy" to your list of cooking terms.**)

Place the slice of American cheese on top of the Thousand Island dressing you just spread.

Cut a slice of ham to fit the size of your

bread and lay it on top of the American cheese.

Place thin slices of pickle or sweet onion on top of the ham if you decided to use them.

Place the slice of Swiss cheese on top.

Spread the top slice of bread with a thin layer of Thousand Island dressing.

Place the second slice of bread on top of the Swiss cheese, dressing side down.

Spread softened butter on top of your sandwich.

Make as many Grilled Ham and Double Cheese Sandwiches as you need for your guests.

Depending on how many sandwiches you made, put a helping or two of butter on your griddle or in your frying pan. Then preheat it at MEDIUM HIGH heat.

When the butter on the griddle or in the frying pan has melted and is preheated, fry your sandwiches, uncovered, until the bottom turns golden brown. (*You can test this by lifting it with a spatula and peeking at the bottom.*)

When one side is golden brown, flip the sandwich over, add more butter to the pan or griddle if needed, and fry the other side until it's golden brown.

Remove the sandwiches from the frying

pan or griddle, cut them into pieces with a sharp knife, arrange the pieces on a plate, and serve immediately.

This sandwich goes well with piping-hot mugs of soup or a generous helping of coleslaw.

CHAPTER FIVE

"Dad!"

Hannah sat bolt upright in bed and stared at the familiar shape that had materialized at the foot of her bed. "What are you doing here? You're . . . you're . . . I thought that you were . . ." Unable to say that awful, final word, she fell silent, merely staring at her father.

"Dead? I am, but they let me come here to be your Ghost of Christmas Past tonight."

"Then you're a . . . a ghost?"

"That's right. They're only going to let me maintain my human shape for a few more minutes. They wanted you to recognize me so that you wouldn't be frightened."

A million questions flew through Hannah's mind, and she turned to look at Moishe. He was staring at her with his one good eye and totally ignoring her father. Hannah turned back to look at her father

again and found that he had been trans-
formed into a white, amorphous shape that
was hovering near the foot of her bed. "But,
Dad . . . Moishe's not even looking at you.
I thought cats could see ghosts."

"Some can, some can't," her father replied. "It's pretty obvious that you have a
cat who can't."

Hannah smiled. Her dad had said, *a cat
who can't,* rather than *a cat that can't.* It
meant that her dad thought of Moishe as a
person, just the way she did.

"I must be dreaming," Hannah said,
considering the possibility.

"No, you're not dreaming. Throw something at me and see what happens."

"No, Dad! I don't want to hurt you!"

"You can't hurt me. I'm already dead.
Pick up that pen you have on your night
table and peg it straight at me. I taught you
how to pitch, remember?"

"I remember," Hannah answered with a
smile.

"Go ahead. Throw a strike. You used to be
pretty good at that."

"No, I wasn't. You're just being nice."

"You caught me on that one, Honey-
bear."

Hannah felt a rush of wonderful memo-
ries. Her dad had called her Honey-bear,

the childhood nickname he'd used for her until Delores had informed him that Hannah was too old to have a nickname like that.

"Maybe you weren't the greatest pitcher in the world," her dad went on, "but you could hit a home run if you were mad enough at the opposing pitcher. Come on, Hannah. Do it. I don't have that much time here."

She'd always obeyed her father when he'd given her a direct order, and Hannah wasn't about to falter now. She picked up the pen, threw it directly at what she thought was the middle of the amorphous shape, and watched in astonishment as the pen passed directly through it and clattered to the floor near her closet.

"Do you believe me now?" he asked her.

Hannah nodded. And then she spoke aloud because she wasn't sure he'd noticed. "Yes, Dad. I believe you now."

"I love you, Hannah. I have to go soon, but they sent me here to give you a glimpse into your past. I hope it does the trick for you."

Hannah was about to ask which trick her father was talking about when his shape spread out flat, like a movie screen that was hanging on the wall. And as she watched, an image appeared.

There Hannah was in the bar of the Corner Tavern, sitting on a stool with her club soda in front of her. The man beside her got up to follow the waitress to his table, and that was when Bonnie came over to sit next to her.

The camera, or perhaps it was her eyes, traveled over to the stool that Bonnie had vacated. She was checking to make sure that Bonnie hadn't left anything behind. There was nothing on the bar in front of Bonnie's stool, and nothing on the floor except the sawdust the staff at the Corner Tavern spread out every morning after the floor was washed and swept. There were two foot-prints from Bonnie's shoes, but nothing else.

"Show's over," her father said as the screen coalesced into his amorphous shape again. "I love you, Honey-bear. If I'm lucky, they might let me come back again. You're scheduled for three ghosts just like the ones in the play. The difference is that we don't need makeup or costumes. We're really ghosts, and we don't rely on special effects and fake turkeys. Now go back to sleep like my good girl, and try to remember what I showed you when I visited you."

Hannah's eyelids felt suddenly heavy, almost as if they were weighted. She wanted to stay awake to see her dad leave, but it was impossible. She rolled over, reached out to pet Moishe's soft fur, and smiled as she slipped into a deep, restful sleep.

Hannah awakened to the scent of hot, strong coffee and something enticing that she couldn't identify. She sat up in bed, dislodging the cat who'd been sleeping on the pillow next to her head, and felt around under the bed for her slippers.

"Rowww!" Moishe complained as she thrust her feet into her slippers and got out of bed.

"I know. I don't really want to get up either, but something smells really good! Michelle must be making breakfast."

That comment elicited a purr from her feline friend. Moishe loved Michelle, especially after all the treats she'd brought with her. He'd even gotten some ham from last night's sandwiches, one of his favorite meats, and several fish-shaped, salmon-flavored treats that Michelle had given him before she'd gone to bed.

"Gingerbread!" Hannah exclaimed aloud as she thrust her arms into the sleeves of the gently worn chenille robe that she'd found at Helping Hands, the local thrift store. "At least I *think* it's gingerbread. It smells like gingerbread, and I can't think of what else it could be."

Moishe did not offer his opinion as he followed Hannah down the carpeted hallway, taking an occasional swipe at the hem of her robe.

When they reached the kitchen, Hannah took one step inside the doorway and into her brightly lit kitchen, sniffed the air again, and stared at her sister, who was standing at the stove. "Not gingerbread?" she asked.

"What?" Michelle looked puzzled.

"Not gingerbread. I thought you were baking gingerbread, but the oven's not on. What are you frying?"

Michelle looked pleased. "You're close, Hannah. I'm frying Gingerbread Pancakes. One of my housemates got the recipe from her grandmother. She said her grandmother used to make Gingerbread Pancakes every Christmas morning and that it was a family tradition. Since it's the Christmas season, I thought it was the perfect time for us to try them."

"They smell really good," Hannah complimented her sister. "What kind of syrup do you use on Gingerbread Pancakes?"

"I don't know, and my friend didn't know, either. She thought maybe her grandmother had served them with honey, but she couldn't really remember."

"We can experiment with syrups," Hannah suggested, heading for the coffeepot to pour herself a cup. "It looks like you're making a lot of pancakes. Are you expecting anyone else for breakfast?"

"No, but my friend told me that her grandmother used to freeze her pancakes and then reheat them in the oven between sheets of foil. That sounded interesting and I thought I'd try it to see if it works."

"If it does, you could probably reheat them in the microwave, too. The only problem is that you can't use foil."

"You wouldn't have to use foil. You could reheat one pancake on a paper plate if you covered it with a paper towel. I've done that with frozen waffles before."

Hannah smiled at her sister. "You're right, and that would be an easy way to make breakfast on the run. You could thaw a pancake, butter it and sprinkle it with sugar, roll it up in a paper towel the way Great-grandmother Elsa used to do with *lefse,* and heat it in the microwave. Then you could eat it on your way to school, or the bus stop, or work."

"We'll try that to see if it works. But in the meantime, would you like a couple of Gingerbread Pancakes? This batch on the

106

griddle is almost ready."

"Of course I would! You're the princess of breakfasts, Michelle."

"Thanks. I'll bring the pancakes to you when they're done, along with the honey, dark Karo syrup, butter and sugar, and molasses. We can try them out and see which topping is best."

In less than five minutes, Hannah had finished her second pancake. She was about to tell Michelle that she liked the molasses best when she thought of something she had to do. She got up to take a new spiral stenographer's pad from her kitchen drawer, grabbed the pen she'd found on the floor of her bedroom, and flipped to the first page.

"Is that your murder book?" Michelle asked.

"Yes." Hannah wrote the name *Phyllis Bates* on the first page. "Do you remember Phyllis Bates from school, Michelle?"

"Vaguely. She was the head cheerleader for the basketball team, wasn't she?"

"Yes."

"And for football, too?"

"That's right. And don't forget baseball."

"She was the blonde with a ponytail?"

"That's right. I know you were still in grade school, but do you remember your impression of her?"

"I *do* remember. Phyllis Bates was a bimbo."

"A *bimbo*?" Hannah repeated Michelle's words in the form of a question.

"Yes. And that was before I even knew what the word *bimbo* meant. Andrea called her that, so I did too. Andrea hated Phyllis Bates."

"How do you know that?"

"She told me so."

"But why?"

"Because Andrea knew I was too scared to tell anyone else."

"Not that. I mean . . . do you know why Andrea hated Phyllis?"

"Yes. It's because Andrea had a crush on Ryan Edwards, the football player that Phyllis was dating at the time."

"Good heavens! How old was Andrea then?"

Michelle shrugged. "Maybe seventh grade? I know Andrea was still in junior high because I had Mrs. Carlson in third grade, and she was Ryan's aunt. Andrea threatened to kill me if I ever mentioned anything about it in school. She would have, too. Andrea was scary when she was mad, and that would have made her really mad."

Hannah looked down at her steno pad. She supposed she should write down Andrea's name as a suspect, but all that was a long time ago and she was sure that Andrea hadn't harbored a grudge against Phyllis for over ten years.

"I *do* know somebody that hated Phyllis, though."

"Who?" Hannah was surprised. Michelle had been back in Lake Eden less than twenty-four hours, and she'd already heard more gossip than Hannah had.

"Mayor Bascomb, that's who. Mother told me all about it. And the mayor's got a really good motive."

Hannah picked up her pen again. "Tell me."

"Okay. Mother took me to Beau Monde to buy me a new jacket before she dropped me off here. She said my old jacket was disreputable."

"That sounds like Mother."

"I know. The new one she bought me is a nice jacket, though. And she got me a new pair of jeans, too."

"That's nice. Now tell me how you know that Mayor Bascomb had a motive."

"I heard Mother and Claire talking about it while I was trying on jeans. The mayor dumped Phyllis when she asked him to set her up in her own furnished condo. And Phyllis got even with him by telling Stephanie Bascomb that she'd been having an affair with the mayor."

Hannah didn't hesitate. She wrote Mayor Bascomb's name on her list of suspects. "Did you hear any other gossip while you were there in the dressing room?"

"No, but I'm willing to bet that Claire knows more. And if she doesn't she can find out. She told Mother that Stephanie bought a whole new wardrobe from her. And Claire said that she had to alter everything before this afternoon because Stephanie was coming in to make sure everything fit."

The wheels in Hannah's mind were churning so fast, she could almost feel a breeze near the top of her head. It didn't take long for her to formulate a plan, and she began to smile.

"What?" Michelle asked, noticing the smile.

"I think we'll have to pay a visit to Beau Monde this afternoon. I'd like to try on a couple of outfits."

"You'd *like* to try on clothing? Come on, Hannah. Everybody knows that you hate to . . ." Michelle stopped and rolled her eyes. "Never mind. I get it. We're going to drop by a few minutes before Stephanie is due to come in?"

"That's the general idea. Let's drop by

Claire's shop before The Cookie Jar opens. Claire probably knows what time Stephanie plans to come in."

"And if Claire doesn't know, maybe she can call to arrange a time," Michelle suggested.

"Exactly right." Hannah got up from the table, rinsed off her plate, and put it in the dishwasher. "Go get your jacket, Michelle."

"Okay. Are we going where I think we're going?"

"You'd better believe it! Claire's probably at the shop early, working on Stephanie's alterations."

"Do you want me to take Claire some pancakes for breakfast? I know she's got a microwave in her back room and I can reheat them for her."

"That's a great idea. And don't forget to bring some toppings, too. Claire's got a real sweet tooth."

GINGERBREAD PANCAKES

1 large egg

1 teaspoon vanilla extract

1/4 cup molasses (**Michelle used Grandma's**)

1 and 1/2 cups water

1 teaspoon ground ginger

1 teaspoon cinnamon

1/4 teaspoon ground cardamom (**if you don't have it, just add a little more cinnamon**)

1/4 teaspoon nutmeg (**freshly grated is best, of course**)

1 and 1/2 cups all-purpose flour (**pack it down in the cup when you measure it**)

1/4 teaspoon baking soda

1 teaspoon baking powder

1/2 teaspoon salt

In a small bowl, whisk a large egg with the vanilla extract.

Add the quarter-cup of molasses and whisk that in.

Add the cup and a half of water and whisk that in.

Hannah's 1st Note: You'll be adding the spices next, but Michelle says that's easier if you mix them together first. She uses a disposable paper bowl. Then you can add the spice mixture to your

egg mixture all at once.

Combine the ground ginger, cinnamon, cardamom, and nutmeg. Stir them around until they're mixed.

Add the spice mixture to your egg mixture and whisk everything together until they're thoroughly combined.

Hannah's 2nd Note: Michelle says to remind you to rinse off your whisk and put it in the sink. If you let the egg dry on the whisk, it's really difficult to get clean.

Get out your favorite stirring spoon. You'll be using it from here on out.

In a larger mixing bowl, combine the flour, baking soda, baking powder, and salt. Mix them until they're well incorporated.

Add the egg mixture to the flour mixture and stir until just incorporated. The batter may be a little lumpy. That's okay. You'll stir it again before you fry it.

Hannah's 3rd Note: If you've made pancakes from scratch before, you know that they're tastier if you "season" them by covering the mixing bowl with plastic wrap and refrigerating the batter overnight. This is why I always mix my batter the night before.

When you're ready to fry your pancakes, prepare your griddle or your frying pan by oiling it before you heat it, or using a mixture with equal parts of oil and butter.

Set your heat at MEDIUM-HIGH. You can test your frying surface to see when it's ready by putting a few drops of water on the surface. If the droplets of water skitter around and then evaporate, your pan is the right temperature to fry pancakes.

If you're using a griddle, you may want to pour on your pancakes rather than use a spoon. Simply transfer the batter to a pitcher and use that to pour. If you'd prefer to dip a large spoon or a small cup into the bowl and transfer the batter to the griddle or the frying pan that way, that's fine, too. (**Michelle used my** *quarter-cup plastic measure that has a little spout on the side. I measured this once, and when she empties the cup of batter in the frying pan, approximately 3 Tablespoons come out of the measuring cup.*)

Fry your pancakes until they're puffed and they look a bit dry around the edges. If you look closely, little bubbles will form at the edges. If you're not sure they're done, lift one edge with a spatula and take a peek. It will be golden brown on the bottom when it's ready to flip.

Turn your pancakes and wait for the other side to fry. Again, you can test your pancake by lifting it slightly with a spatula and peeking to see if it's golden brown.

If you don't have people sitting at your table waiting to eat breakfast, you can fry all your pancakes now and keep them warm until everyone comes to the table by separating them with layers of foil or paper towels, placing them in a 9-inch by 13-inch cake pan, covering the pan loosely with another piece of foil, and keeping them in a warm oven set at the lowest temperature.

Serve with plenty of soft butter and your choice of honey, dark Karo syrup, or molasses. These Gingerbread Pancakes are also good buttered, spread with jam, and topped with a dollop of sour cream.

CHAPTER SIX

"Keep your eye on the time," Hannah advised as she took another batch of cookies from the industrial oven at The Cookie Jar and placed the cookie sheets on shelves in the baker's rack. "We have to get to Claire's before Stephanie does, or our plan won't work."

"We've still got an hour," Michelle replied. "And I'm ready with a batch of Angel Jellies that we can bake first."

"Good, they're a favorite out front. Which flavor?"

"Raspberry. You had a whole big jar of seedless raspberry jam." Michelle stopped speaking and walked a bit closer to the swinging restaurant-type door that separated the kitchen from the coffee shop. "Lisa must be telling the story of the murder again. There's not a peep from any of the customers out there, and we've been packed ever since we opened this morning."

"I know. Everyone loves to hear Lisa tell stories. She keeps the customers mesmerized."

"And eating cookies," Michelle reminded her.

"That's right. It makes me feel a little strange to say it, but Lake Eden murders are good for our business."

Michelle raised up on tiptoe so she could see through the high window in the door. "She's got them all on the edges of their seats. Babs Dubinski is leaning forward so far, it's a wonder she doesn't tip over. And Grandma Knudson has her hand cupped around her ear so she doesn't miss a word. Lisa's a great storyteller, Hannah. She really ought to try out for the Lake Eden Players. I'll bet Tory Bascomb would love to have her."

"Agreed. Lisa could be the star of every show. She's a better actress than anyone else in town."

The phone on the kitchen wall rang, and Michelle hurried to answer it. They'd promised to answer the phone while Lisa was performing.

"The Cookie Jar," Michelle informed the caller. "This is Michelle speaking." She listened for a few moments, and then she said, "I'll tell her, Mother. Does Lisa know yet?" There was another moment of silence, and then Michelle laughed. "You might know that the Lake Eden Gossip Hotline would get it first. And he's on his way here now to tell her?" There was a pause, and then Michelle spoke again. "Okay, Mother. Thanks for telling us. We'll give Lisa a heads-up."

"What?" Hannah asked, the moment that Michelle had hung up the phone.

"That was Mother. Mayor Bascomb is on the way over here to tell Lisa that she's the new Mrs. Claus."

"How did Mother know that?"

"Luanne's mother was cleaning Mayor Bascomb's office this morning, and she heard him mention it on the phone to Rod McRae. She called Luanne from her cell phone to tell her, and Mother just happened to be at Granny's Attic when Luanne took the call. Mother asked Luanne what Mrs. Hanks wanted, and Luanne told her all about it. Mother figures she knew less than five minutes after Mayor Bascomb ended his call to Rod and hung up the phone."

"That's fast, even for the Lake Eden Gossip Hotline. The news on those jungle drums travels fast."

Michelle's eyebrows shot up. "Don't tell me you got up in the middle of the night to watch *Jungle Drums* on the old movie channel!"

Hannah sighed. "I did, but it didn't start out that way. I watched *Scrooge,* the nineteen fifty-one film with Alistair Sim. But I still wasn't sleepy so I stayed up to see what would come on next."

"And it was *Jungle Drums*?"

"Yes."

"And you actually watched it?"

"Yes, but I fell asleep about halfway through."

"That was probably a blessing. I can't believe you watched that long!"

"I didn't want to," Hannah admitted. "I really wanted to change the channel, but the remote was on the other side of the couch and I didn't want to disturb Moishe. He was sitting in my lap, purring so loudly that I could barely hear the dialogue."

"Moishe did you a favor. You should give him a shrimp. What woke you up in the first place?"

"Nothing *woke* me. I couldn't get to sleep in the first place. When I went to bed, I started thinking about Phyllis and who might have killed her. I was so busy going through lists of suspects in my head that I couldn't fall asleep."

"So you made yourself a cup of hot chocolate with miniature marshmallows, settled down on the couch with Moishe, and flicked on the television."

"That's right. I think you know me too well, Michelle."

"Maybe I do, but that doesn't mean I love you any less." Michelle smiled at Hannah. "I'll go out front and ask Lisa to come back here right after she does the crowd reaction. I think she's just about at that point in her story, but I'll check it out to make sure."

Both Hannah and Michelle moved closer to the door, where they could hear Lisa's voice.

"She saw a mound at the bottom of the snow-covered ditch, a mound the same size as a body. She didn't want to think that way, but you know Hannah. Anyone else would have climbed back up to the top of the ditch just as fast as they could and run back inside to get help. But not our Hannah. Do you think she hesitated?"

"No!" the crowd in the coffee shop chorused.

"Of course she didn't hesitate," a male voice called out and Hannah knew exactly who it was. *"Hannah's got slaydar!"*

"Mike?" Michelle asked.

"Who else?" Hannah confirmed it.

"I've heard Lisa tell this story twice, and

she's winding down now," Michelle informed her. "I'll go out and give her the high sign."

"Do you think she'll know what you mean?"

"She'll know." Michelle sounded certain. "Lisa and I worked out a series of hand signals right after the last Lake Eden murder. If I stand at the back of the house and run my finger across my throat, it means I want her to end her story as soon as she can. And when I beckon to her and point toward the kitchen, she'll know that we want her to come back here right after she finishes."

Hannah glanced at the clock on the kitchen wall. "Okay. Go ahead. Marge, and Lisa's dad, should be here by now, and they can handle the coffee shop."

After Michelle had left, Hannah placed the trays of unbaked Angel Jellies inside the industrial oven. She had set the timer, poured herself a fresh cup of coffee, and taken a stool at the stainless-steel workstation when Michelle came back from the coffee shop.

"Lisa read my signal," she reported. "She should be here in a moment or two."

"Good. I don't want her to be caught unaware when Mayor Bascomb comes in."

"You don't think Lisa will turn down a chance to play Mrs. Claus, do you?"

"No. She really wanted to be Mrs. Claus. She mentioned it to me a couple of times. The only reason she might hesitate is if she thinks I can't handle the concession stand alone."

"You don't have to handle anything alone with me here," Michelle pointed out. "I'll help you, and Lisa can play Mrs. Claus. That should make Herb happy, too."

Hannah thought about the kiss she'd seen between Phyllis and Herb. "I hope so," she said.

"What's up?" Lisa breezed into the kitchen and took a stool at the workstation.

"Mother called," Hannah told her. "It seems Mayor Bascomb is on his way here to invite you to be this year's Mrs. Claus."

"Really?" Lisa looked both excited and pleased, but then her expression took on a worried look. "Do you think that would be right? I mean, after Phyllis and everything?"

"The show must go on," Michelle reminded her, "and there's nothing you can do about Phyllis. She's dead and she can't play Santa's wife."

"I know, but . . . do you think people will think less of me if I agree so fast? I'm just wondering if it's proper. She's been dead less than a day."

"They won't think less of you, Lisa," Hannah reassured her. "You know that the kids look forward to seeing Santa and Mrs. Claus every year. Their parents will be grateful that you agreed to step in and play the part."

"Well . . . there *is* that," Lisa conceded. "I'd hate to disappoint the children. But I'll have to get into my costume at intermission so I'm ready in time. Do you think you can handle the candy sales?"

"I'll help Hannah," Michelle spoke up. "I already told her that I would. This is important, Lisa. Santa and Mrs. Claus have appeared at the end of the Christmas play for as long as I can remember. I used to sit on Santa's lap when Santa was Earl Flensburg. And I loved it when Mrs. Claus handed me my gift bag of treats. Herb can't do it alone, and he needs you. You almost have to do it."

"Well, yes. You're right. I do." Lisa looked pleased at the prospect of playing Mrs. Claus.

"You're the natural choice," Hannah added. "Everyone knows that you're Herb's wife. And now you also get to play his pretend wife on stage."

"Lisa?" Marge poked her head into the

kitchen. "Mayor Bascomb is here, and he says he needs to talk to you."

"Of course. Please get him a cup of coffee and some cookies, Marge. And tell him I'll be right out." Lisa waited until Marge had left, and then she turned to Hannah. "I just thought of something. Is Mayor Bascomb one of your suspects?"

"Actually . . . yes. He certainly had a motive. Phyllis told his wife what was going on between them when he refused to set Phyllis up in a condo. And Stephanie made him pay for his mistake in designer clothes and expensive gems. I'd call that a motive, wouldn't you?"

Lisa nodded. "Yes, I would. So you think that the mayor might have killed Phyllis to get even?"

"There are worse motives," Hannah said. "Anger is a powerful emotion."

"So now all you have to do is find out if he had the opportunity . . . is that right?"

"That's right. If he has an alibi, he's in the clear. If he doesn't, he's still on my suspect list."

"And Herb's on there too, especially if he noticed me leaving the auditorium after that kiss Phyllis gave him. Is that right?"

Hannah felt like groaning, but she didn't. Lisa always went straight to the heart of the matter. "That's right. I'm sorry Lisa. I don't really think that Herb did it, but . . ."

"But he had a motive. And we don't know if he had the opportunity because we don't know where he was until after midnight last night."

This time Hannah did groan. "I don't like it Lisa. But Herb's on my suspect list."

"And I'm there, too. I have to be. I have a perfect motive. After that kiss, I was so jealous, I couldn't see straight. I told you that I had to go home to feed the dogs, but you have no way of knowing if I actually did that, or not. Maybe I drove straight out to the Corner Tavern, spotted Phyllis getting out of her car, and killed her in a jealous fit of rage."

"But you *couldn't* have killed her. You were wearing ankle boots. I saw them. And you couldn't have climbed down into that ditch wearing ankle boots. You would have come in with soaked feet, and you didn't. I looked down at your boots when we were standing there in the parking lot. They're light-colored suede, and they weren't wet."

"Maybe I wasn't wearing ankle boots then. Maybe I had another pair of boots in the trunk and I used those. You don't know that I didn't. You didn't check, and neither did anyone else."

"Lisa!" Michelle sounded very upset. "Cut it out! You just gave yourself a motive and admitted that you had the opportunity!"

"I know that, but Hannah would have thought of that eventually, if it hasn't already occurred to her." Lisa turned back to Hannah. "I'm on your suspect list too, aren't I?"

Hannah visibly winced, but there was no reason to lie about it. "Yes, Lisa. You're on it. But I don't really think that you . . ."

"That doesn't matter," Lisa interrupted her. "You have to investigate me, too. That's one of the things I like best about you, Hannah. You're fair. I can tell you right now that I didn't do it, but that doesn't count for anything. Mike's going to zero in on me, too. He's a good cop, and he's bound to investigate me. I'm just hoping that you'll hurry and clear both Herb and me by catching the real killer. You'll do that, won't you?"

"I'll certainly do my best," Hannah promised.

"That's good enough for me. Now I'd better get out there and hear what Mayor Bascomb has to say to me. And I'd better help you either clear him or finger him."

Michelle and Hannah were silent for a moment after the swinging door had shut behind Lisa. Then Michelle shook her head.

"*Finger him?* That dates back a couple of decades. Where did Lisa ever hear a phrase like that?"

"*Dragnet.* She told me that she watches reruns while she's waiting for Herb to come home. He's been working really late almost every night this month."

"Do you think he's really working?"

"I don't know, but I'm going to find out."

There was a knock on the back kitchen door, and Michelle turned to Hannah. "Mother?" she asked.

"No. Mother's knock is more impatient and she generally knocks in threes."

"Threes?"

"Yes. Knock-knock-knock. And then knock-knock-knock again. After that, she tries the door. And if it's unlocked, she comes in."

"How about Mike? He always checks in with you the day after a murder."

"It's not Mike. We heard him out front in the coffee shop."

"Unless he left and walked around to the back door."

"No." Hannah shook her head. "It's definitely not Mike. He always knocks like he's serving a search warrant. It's loud and demanding and staccato. I think it's probably Norman. He's got a firm knock, but

127

it's not as commanding as Mike's and not as impatient as Mother's. Go let him in, will you please? I'll pour him a cup of coffee and get him settled at the workstation."

ANGEL JELLIES

Preheat oven to 275 degrees F., rack in the center position.

(*That's two hundred and seventy-five degrees F., not a misprint.*)

6 large eggs
1/4 teaspoon cream of tartar
1/2 teaspoon vanilla extract
1/4 teaspoon salt
1 cup white (*granulated*) sugar
2 Tablespoons (*1/8 cup*) all-purpose flour
(*Pack it down when you measure it.*)
a little flour in a small bowl for later
a small jar of seedless raspberry jam (*or your favorite jam if you don't like raspberry*)

Hannah's 1st Note: Make sure you use jam and not jelly in this recipe. I know the name is Angel Jellies, but that's because "Angel Jams" didn't sound as nice. I haven't tried jelly, but there's more liquid in jelly than in jam. Jam has pieces of fruit in it and although the liquid in jam will melt, those pieces of fruit won't melt. Jelly could melt and leak out of the bottoms of the cookies as they bake, making them soggy.

Separate 6 large eggs and put the whites in one container and the yolks in another.

Cover the container with the yolks and put it in the refrigerator. You can use it to make yolk-rich scrambled eggs for breakfast in the morning, or a yolk-rich Chocolate Flan with Caramel Whipped Cream for dessert.

Set the whites on your kitchen counter until they've come up to room temperature. (*This will give them more volume when you whip them.*)

Prepare your cookie sheets by lining them with parchment paper (*this works best*) or brown parcel-wrapping paper if you don't have parchment. Spray the paper with Pam or another non-stick cooking spray and dust it lightly with flour.

Hannah's 2nd Note: You can also use Pam Baking Spray or another brand of baking spray that has flour in it.

Hannah's 3rd Note: These cookies are a lot easier to make if you use an electric mixer because you must beat the egg whites until they form soft peaks and, ultimately, stiff peaks. You can use a copper bowl and a whisk, but it will take some time and muscle.

Beat the egg whites with the cream of tartar, vanilla, and salt until they are firm enough to hold a soft peak. Test this by shutting off the mixer and dotting the egg whites with the side of a clean rubber spatula. When you pull up the spatula, a soft peak should form.

Hannah's 4th Note: For those of you who haven't made meringues before, soft peaks slump a bit and bend over on themselves. That's what you want at this stage. A bit later on in the recipe, you'll want stiff peaks. Those stand straight up and do not slump or bend over.

With the mixer running on MEDIUM HIGH speed, sprinkle the egg white mixture with approximately one third of the sugar. Turn the mixer up to HIGH speed for ten seconds. Then turn the mixer down to MEDIUM HIGH speed again.

Sprinkle in half of the remaining sugar, turn the mixer up to HIGH speed for ten seconds, and then back down to MEDIUM HIGH speed.

Sprinkle in the remaining sugar and follow the same procedure, turning the mixer up to HIGH speed for ten seconds, or until stiff peaks form. Then turn OFF the mixer completely.

Sprinkle in the flour and mix it into the egg white mixture at LOW speed. You don't want to whip any air out of the meringue.

Take the bowl out of the mixer, give it a gentle stir with your rubber spatula, and place it next to your prepared cookie sheet.

Use a spoon to drop small mounds of dough on your cookie sheet, no more than 12 dough mounds to a standard-sized sheet. *(If you make 4 rows with 3 dough mounds in each row, that should be perfect.)*

Hannah's 5th Note: The mound of dough should be no larger than a ping pong ball. (If you've never played table tennis, this is a little smaller than a golf ball. If you've never played golf, make the dough mounds the size of a large walnut in the shell. If you've never seen a large walnut in the shell, you'd better ask someone or you won't have a clue!)

Dip the pad of your impeccably clean finger in the flour. *(I use my pointer finger.)* Make an indentation in the center of your mounds of cookie dough, dipping your finger in the bowl of flour before indenting each mound. Make sure your indentations DO NOT go all the way to the bottom of the dough mounds. *(If the jam leaks out in the oven, it'll go all over and you certainly don't want that!)*

Use the tip of a small spoon to take a little jam from the jar and deposit it inside the indentation you made. Don't use too much jam. A little will do just fine.

Drop a little mound of cookie dough over the top of the jam to cover it completely. Then it will be a lovely surprise when everyone bites into your cookies.

Bake your Angel Jellies at 275 degrees F. for approximately 40 minutes or until the meringue part of the cookie is lightly golden and dry to the touch when you tap it lightly with your finger.

Take the Angel Jellies out of the oven. Cool the cookies on the paper-lined baking sheet by setting it on a cold stovetop burner or on a wire rack.

When your Angel Jellies are completely cool, peel them off the paper and store them in an airtight container in a cool, dry place. (*Unfortunately, your refrigerator is NOT a dry place. A cupboard shelf will do just fine as long as it's not near your stove.*)

Yield: 3 to 4 dozen crunchy, melt-in-your-mouth cookies with a delightful surprise in the center. Warning: Angel Jellies are like potato chips. You can't eat just one!

Michelle's Note: My college housemates love these cookies. I've made them with strawberry jam, peach jam, apricot jam, pineapple jam, blueberry jam, and orange marmalade.

CHAPTER SEVEN

"Norman!" Hannah greeted him with a cup of coffee, a plate of cookies, and a smile. "How are you? I haven't seen you in a while."

Norman stood up as she placed the coffee and cookies in front of him and pulled her into his arms to give her a hug. "I know I haven't dropped in for a while. I've been busy at the house, directing workmen. And I've gone out to the mall every night for Christmas shopping. How about you?"

"Here," Hannah replied with a sigh. "Christmas and Valentine's Day are our busy times. And this year we're doing all the cookies and candy for the children's Christmas gift bags."

"Christmas is always a busy time. I hired Doc Bennett to take over for me until after the first of the year. He needs the work, and I need time off."

"Are you going away for the holidays?"

Hannah asked him.

"Not a chance. I'm doing some construction at the house."

"What construction? I thought you loved the house the way we designed it."

"Oh, I do. But things have changed and I wanted to update. Do you know that you can buy a humungous LED big screen now?"

"I hadn't noticed. I'm perfectly happy with the television I have now."

"I'm not. You know those old movies you love, Hannah?"

Hannah began to smile. "You mean the old romantic comedies and the chick flicks?"

"Yes. And the old detective films. They're all remastered now. And I needed to enlarge the den so that I could get a hundred-and-twenty-inch screen on the wall without being crowded."

Hannah's mouth dropped open. "But . . . that's practically theater-sized!"

"That's right. And won't it be fun to watch our favorite classic films in a home theater with perfect surround sound and incredibly comfortable seating?"

"Maybe," Hannah said, but she couldn't hide her delighted expression. She loved to watch classic movies with Norman.

"Then you'll come out to watch films with

me when my home theater is finished?"

Hannah's timing was perfect. She waited a beat before she answered. But when Norman started to look a little nervous, she relented. "Yes. You can bet I'll be there!"

"Wonderful!"

Norman looked very happy, and Hannah felt a little guilty about what she had planned to say next. But that didn't stop her. "You bet I'll come! But only if you've got a popcorn machine."

Norman's smile grew larger by the nanosecond. "I knew you'd say that!"

"I'm that predictable?"

"No, it's just that I know you so well. And because I know you that well, I've got one."

"You have a popcorn machine?"

"Yes. I bought one just so I could say I had it. Of course I don't know how to work it yet, but . . ."

"I'll figure it out," Hannah cut in. "When I was in high school, I made popcorn for every movie they ran in the auditorium. And when I got to college, I made popcorn in the big theater, the small theater, the concession stand for football, basketball, and baseball games, and any other special events where they thought they could make a profit selling it. There's not a popcorn machine on the face of this earth that I can't learn to operate."

"This one's digital."

"Ooooh! Fun! I've never seen a digital popcorn machine before. And that reminds me . . . is it portable?"

Norman looked slightly confused. "Actually . . . yes. It doesn't weigh that much. And it makes a ton of popcorn."

"You saved my life," Hannah told him.

"Okay." Norman's eyes narrowed. "How did I do that? Or will I be sorry I asked?"

"You may be sorry, especially when you have to lug that popcorn machine all the way over to Jordan High."

It took Norman a moment, but then he gave a nod. "I get it. Their popcorn machine is broken again, and you need one for the concession stand at the Christmas play. Am I on the right track?"

"Not only are you on the right track, you won the race! Will you lend it to me, Norman? It's just for three nights. Michelle and I are manning the concession stand at the play because Lisa's going to be Mrs. Claus. The Lake Eden Players usually borrow Jordan High's machine, but theirs is broken and the new one they ordered won't be here until after the holidays."

"You can borrow mine on one condition."

"What's the one condition?"

"It's simple. You have to teach me how to use it and let me make the popcorn for you. You and Michelle will be busy enough selling everything else. I want to help."

"Then you've got a job," Hannah said happily, reaching out to take his hand. "Thanks, Norman. You always come through for me in a pinch."

Norman gave her hand a gentle squeeze, and then he looked very serious. "Are you doing it again, Hannah?"

Hannah's first instinct was to ask him what he meant, but she already knew exactly what he was asking. "Yes," she admitted. "Lisa's a suspect and so is Herb. I have to clear them."

"By catching the real killer?"

"That's the plan. Lisa doesn't have an alibi for a critical period of time last night. She was with me until nine, and then she went home alone to feed Dillon and Sammy. She didn't join me again until around ten at the Corner Tavern."

"And Herb?"

"Herb told Lisa that he's been working late, but . . ." Hannah's voice trailed off. She really shouldn't be discussing Lisa's marital problems with Norman.

"But what?" Norman prompted.

Hannah sighed. "But Lisa has her doubts."

138

"Let me get this straight. You want me to find an alibi for both Lisa and Herb?"

"That's right. An alibi for one would be good. And an alibi for both would be even better."

"Okay. I'll keep my eyes and ears open. Do you know the time of death?"

"Not yet. Doc can't tell exactly, but he always puts a window of time in the autopsy report. My problem is, I don't have the autopsy report yet."

"It shouldn't be long now."

Hannah was puzzled. "What are you talking about?"

"I saw your mother on the highway when I drove to town. She was heading in the opposite direction, and unless she was going out to the mall three hours before it opens, she was heading out to the hospital."

"What time was that?"

"And hour or so ago. I stopped at Hal and Rose's for breakfast, dropped in at the office to go over the mail, and then I came over here."

"Perfect. Mother should be here any . . ." Hannah stopped speaking as they heard a series of knocks at the door. "There she is now."

"Do you want me to get that?" Michelle asked from the other side of the kitchen.

139

"Yes, please," Hannah answered. "It's Mother."

"On my way, Hannah. I'll let her in, pour her some coffee, and then I'll put more cookies on the plate I was fixing for you and Norman. Mother loves these Angel Jellies, and they're cool enough to eat now."

A second or two later, Delores came in. She took a stool next to Norman at the workstation and plunked a manila envelope in front of Hannah.

"Is that what I think it is?" Hannah asked her.

"Yes, if you think it's the autopsy report." Delores tapped the envelope with one impeccably manicured nail, and smiled smugly. "I assumed that you'd need it?"

"You assumed right. Thank you, Mother. You're wonderful to do this for me."

"I like to help," Delores said modestly, but Hannah noticed that her smug smile was still in place. "And this time I took an extra precaution. I called Andrea last night and told her I was going to get it and she didn't have to sneak it out of Bill's briefcase and scan it before she put it back."

"Was Andrea grateful that you were getting it and she didn't have to?" Hannah asked the question, even though she thought she already knew the answer.

140

"Actually . . . no. I thought she'd be relieved. She takes an awful chance, you know. Bill would be so upset with her if he ever caught her. But she sounded almost . . ."

"Deprived?" Norman provided the word.

"Why, yes! That's right. And all I was trying to do was help."

"Of course you were," Hannah said quickly. "And I'm sure that Andrea realizes that. It's possible you just caught her at a bad time when you called."

Delores thought about that for a moment, and then she gave a little nod. "You're right, dear. I *did* catch her at a bad time. Grandma McCann had taken Tracey and a friend ice skating at the school rink, and Andrea was trying to put Bethie to bed. I heard Bethie say that she wouldn't go to bed without *raffey* and Andrea had no idea what a *raffey* was."

"Does Bethie have a toy giraffe?"

Delores didn't say anything. She just stared at Hannah so intently that Hannah began to feel uncomfortable. "Don't look at me that way, Mother. It was just a guess."

"But you're right! Bethie has a stuffed giraffe and it's one of her favorite toys! You really should have children, Hannah. You have a natural flair for understanding them."

141

A host of replies occurred to Hannah including, *It takes two to have children, Mother!* and *I'll take that under consideration and let you know within a decade or so.* But she knew that anything she said would only make the situation more uncomfortable. And that was when Michelle arrived at the workstation with the platter of Angel Jellies and saved her the necessity of replying.

"Have a cookie, Mother," Michelle invited. "They're raspberry Angel Jellies."

"My favorite!" Delores declared, reaching for one.

"Norman?" Michelle offered the platter to him.

"Thanks, Michelle. I've never had these before."

"Hannah?" Michelle passed the platter to her. And then, in an undertone, she said, "I think you'd better put something in your mouth before you insert your foot."

Hannah had all she could do not to laugh. "Just set the platter in front of Mother, Michelle. She likes these cookies so much."

"Of course. I planned to do that." Michelle took the stool next to Hannah. "What are you giving Andrea and Bill for Christmas, Mother?"

"I don't know yet, dear."

"How about if we all go in on it together

and give Andrea and Bill a few days in a nice hotel, just the two of them?"

"Why, that's a wonderful idea!" Delores agreed immediately. "But you girls don't have to contribute anything. I can afford to do it by myself and I'd like it to be *my* present to them. I wonder which hotel I should choose."

"Somewhere warm," Hannah suggested. "I think the cold is getting to Bill. When he came in the other morning, he was shivering."

"You're right, dear," Delores agreed. "This has been a particularly cold winter. I know that Bill has the week after Christmas off. Andrea mentioned it to me the other day. I could fly them down to Florida to a nice, relaxing resort. They could have a mini second honeymoon."

"That sounds nice," Norman said. "Mother and Earl went to Florida last March, and they loved it."

"Then that's what I'll do. I'll fly them down there the day after Christmas and they can come home the day after New Year's."

"You'd better act fast to get plane tickets," Michelle cautioned her. "Flights are hard to get over holidays."

"I know, dear. Don't worry. I'll rush right

home and do it."

"Before you do that, it might be a good idea to check with Bill to make sure exactly which days he has off," Hannah reminded her. "I could be wrong, but I don't think Andrea would like to go on a mini second honeymoon all by herself."

CHAPTER EIGHT

"Here she comes!" Claire warned.

"Thanks," Hannah replied. She was sitting sideways on a settee in Claire's dressing room with her feet tucked up and her steno pad open to a fresh page in front of her.

"I'm ready," Michelle said from the opposite end of the settee. She'd assumed the same position and also held a notepad in one hand and a pen in the other.

"Come in, Mrs. Bascomb." Claire's voice carried easily to the dressing room. "I have everything all ready for you."

"Good. I don't have much time this afternoon. I'm meeting a friend for afternoon tea, and then Richard and I have a dinner party we must attend. Mayoral duties, you know."

Michelle rolled her eyes up toward the ceiling, and Hannah smiled at her youngest sister. Both of them knew that Stephanie

145

had no plans for tea. If Stephanie was meeting a friend for tea, then *tea* was a euphemism for Stephanie's new favorite drink, a lemon drop vodka martini.

The doorknob on the dressing room rattled as Stephanie tried the door. But Claire had everything under control. "Please use the larger dressing room, Mrs. Bascomb. I've hung your lovely choices in there. The lighting's much better than it is in this one."

"Of course."

Michelle and Hannah heard the door to the adjacent dressing room open and then close again, and Hannah put her finger to her lips. Michelle nodded, and both of them were completely silent as they waited for Claire to engage Stephanie in conversation. Claire knew exactly what they needed to know. They'd gone over it all this morning.

For long moments, there were no sounds except the rustling of cloth and the scratchy sound of zippers being closed. Then, at last, they heard the door to the adjacent dressing room open.

"Claire?" Stephanie Bascomb called out.

"Right here, Mrs. Bascomb," Claire answered. Her voice was a bit louder than Stephanie's, and Hannah realized that Claire must be standing just outside the dressing room where they were hidden.

"What do you think? Is it a bit tight over the hips?"

There was a pause, and Hannah assumed that Claire was assessing the fit.

"No, I think it's perfect," Claire gave her opinion. "Of course, if it makes you uncomfortable, I can always let it out a little over the hips, but I think it looks stunning on you just the way it is. It's too bad you didn't have this last night when you went out to dinner with the mayor."

"Oh, that's all right. We had to cancel anyway. Richard's meeting with the town council lasted until eight-thirty, and our reservations were for eight. We settled for going out for drinks and appetizers with Del Woodley. He's on the council, you know."

"I haven't seen Del in a while. He's well?"

"He seems to be, especially now that Benton has moved to Lake Eden permanently and taken over production at DelRay Manufacturing. Del was working too hard, and after Judith was gone, he had no social life at all."

"But now he does?"

"Oh, yes! Danielle has been very good for him."

This time Hannah did turn to look at Michelle, who appeared every bit as shocked as Hannah was.

"Danielle Watson?" Claire asked.

"Yes. Del called her right after the council meeting and invited her to join us for drinks last night."

"Danielle Watson is dating Del Woodley?"

"Heavens no! *Benton* is dating Danielle. And just between you and me, I think it could be serious. But Benton was still at the plant last night, and Danielle didn't want Del to feel that he was a third wheel. She's a very nice person, you know. She makes sure that Del is included in a lot of their social events. She even acts as a hostess for Del on the rare occasions when Del entertains."

Hannah jotted a note in her book to call Danielle Watson at her dance studio. If drinks with the mayor had lasted any longer than ten-thirty or eleven, Mayor Bascomb was in the clear.

"I'm sorry that you didn't get to go out to dinner, but that still sounds like a nice evening," Claire commented.

"Oh, it was. Richard came to the house to pick me up, and Del was already in the car. I joined them, and then we stopped to pick up Danielle at her dance studio. Richard was going to invite his sister, Tory, to join us but she was tied up with the people from the Christmas play."

"Has Del been dating Tory?" Claire asked, and Hannah felt like applauding. It was precisely the question she would have asked.

"Yes, a few times. They're both very well off, you know. I think both of them are comfortable with each other. Del knows that Tory isn't a gold-digger, and she knows that Del isn't after her money. It's difficult for people with money to find suitable companions, don't you think?"

"Well . . ."

"Of course you wouldn't really know about that," Stephanie cut off any answer that Claire might have given, thereby proving that she didn't give a fig about Claire's opinion on social matters.

"Was it a late evening?" Claire asked Stephanie.

"I didn't notice the time. Why do you ask? Do I look tired?"

"Not at all. You look fresh as a daisy and absolutely fabulous in that lovely outfit."

"Good. I'd better try on another one. We're wasting my time, chatting about inconsequential things."

"Of course," Claire responded quickly. "Try on the claret-colored pantsuit, Mrs. Bascomb. That color is so lovely on you."

"Yes. Isn't it."

It was a statement, not a question, and

Hannah rolled her eyes ceiling-ward. Their mayor's wife was not shy and demure when compliments were offered.

"Come with me, Claire," Stephanie commanded. "I'll need help with those small buttons in the back."

The door to Stephanie's dressing room opened with a click. Hannah listened to the sound of two sets of footfalls entering the dressing room. She waited until the door clicked closed again, and then she turned to motion to Michelle. They had the information they needed, and they could sneak out while Stephanie Bascomb was trying on the pantsuit. And then they could dash back to The Cookie Jar to pick up some kind of sweet treat for Danielle, hurry down the street to her dance studio, and find out exactly what time drinks with the first family of Lake Eden had ended on the previous evening.

When they returned to The Cookie Jar, they found Lisa in the kitchen. "You look like you're in a hurry," she said as they rushed in the door.

"We are," Hannah told her. "Stephanie Bascomb just mentioned that she went out for drinks last night with the mayor. And Del Woodley. And Danielle joined them."

"Claire asked Stephanie what time that was," Michelle added, "but Stephanie didn't remember. My guess is that Stephanie had twee martoonis, or maybe more."

Hannah laughed. "You got that phrase from Dad, didn't you?"

"Yes. It used to crack me up when he said it. I always wanted to use it, but the time was never right . . . until now."

"So rather than go straight to the dance studio, you came back here to get something to take to Danielle," Lisa guessed. "Is that right?"

Michelle looked impressed. "That's very good, Lisa. You figured out Hannah's M.O."

"Of course I did. I've seen her do this before. Hannah always brings something tasty to exchange for information. It's the barter system. She makes people happy and content, and they tell her exactly what she needs to know. And they don't even know they're doing it."

Hannah began to frown slightly. "You're right, Lisa. But it doesn't sound very nice when you put it that way. And . . . actually . . . I've never really thought of it that way before." She stopped and considered it for a moment or two. "It *is* the barter system. Do you think that what I'm doing is wrong?"

"Not at all!" Lisa responded quickly. "You always bring something when you go somewhere. And there's nothing wrong with asking for information. After all, you're trying to catch a murderer."

"And she's trying to prove that the murderer's not you," Michelle added.

Lisa smiled. "There's that, too. I do have a vested interest. And it just so happens I've got the perfect treat for you to take to Danielle."

"What?" Hannah asked.

"You'll see." Lisa hurried to the walk-in cooler, disappeared inside, and returned with a tray of candy. "I happen to know that Danielle loves caramels. Try these and tell me what you think."

Hannah and Michelle each took a piece and bit into it. And then both of them smiled.

"Incredible!" Hannah pronounced.

"You said it!" Michelle took another bite. "These are worth a boatload of information."

"They're the chocolate caramels I told you about yesterday. Marge took over for me out front and I made a batch and stuck them in the cooler. And a couple of hours later, I came back here and wrapped them in wax paper. I hope Danielle likes them.

And I hope she knows something about the murder. It's really unnerving to be a suspect."

"I've never been up here before," Michelle said, as Hannah pulled open the heavy door a few feet from the entrance to the Red Owl Grocery store.

"You'll love it. It was just an empty space until Danielle rented it, but it has big floor-to-ceiling windows in the front and Danielle's walled off part of the back for living quarters."

Hannah led the way up the long, carpeted staircase. As they climbed, she gestured toward the walls. "What do you think?"

"Very clever." Michelle obviously admired the sets of footsteps that diagrammed classic dances, each set depicted in a different color. "Listen, Hannah. I think I hear a waltz."

"You do. Danielle must have an adult class."

As they climbed, the music changed to a polka. "Music for a wedding reception?" Michelle guessed.

"It sounds like it. Danielle mentioned that wedding parties were a big part of her business."

"Because of the first bride and groom dance?"

"Yes, but there's a new trend around Lake Eden. After the bride and groom dance, the whole wedding party gets out there for the next dance. And then the bride's mother dances with the groom's father, and the groom's mother dances with the bride's father."

"That's a lot of dancing. Who started all that anyway?"

Hannah shrugged. "I don't know, but I wouldn't put it past Danielle. She's always looking for ways to increase her business."

The music switched again and a slow dance began to play. It rolled out in a wave to greet them as Hannah opened the studio door. "Let's wait right here in the reception area until Danielle's class is over."

It turned out that they were in luck because right after the slow dance had ended, the music stopped and a few moments later, Danielle's customers began to emerge from the practice room and file out. After Hannah and Michelle had greeted the people they knew and exchanged pleasantries with the ones they didn't, Danielle came out and saw them sitting there.

"Hi, Hannah. Michelle. How are you?"

"We're fine," Hannah said, handing her

the bag Lisa had filled for her. "We brought you something."

"Oooh!" Danielle began to smile as she peeked inside. "Candy! What kind is it?"

"Chocolate caramels that Lisa made."

"I love caramels." Danielle held out the bag. "Would you like one?" she offered.

"We already tested them down at The Cookie Jar," Michelle told her. "We wanted to make sure they were as good as they looked. Do you have a few minutes to talk, Danielle?"

"I have at least a half hour before my next class comes in. Come with me, and I'll put on the coffee." Danielle led them into the interior. They walked through the class area and into her living quarters. It was one large area, almost like an artist's loft, with a bedroom that was cordoned off with a curtain, a living room with a sofa and an easy chair, a tiny bathroom off to the side of the bedroom alcove, and a small, but workable kitchen.

"Sit down." Danielle gestured toward her kitchen table. "I'm sure you're here for a reason, and it's probably not for dance lessons."

"You're right," Hannah told her, noticing the coffee machine on Danielle's counter. "I thought you drank tea, Danielle."

"I do. Benton gave me this machine, and it makes both tea and coffee." She held up a small cup-like pod. "Would you like French roast, Italian roast, or espresso?"

"French roast," Hannah answered, choosing her favorite.

"The same for me," Michelle concurred.

"Just listen," Danielle said as she put a coffee pod into the machine and set an empty cup on the tray below. "It pokes holes in the pod and forces hot water through. And it takes less than a minute."

Hannah and Michelle watched as the machine worked. And less than a minute later, Hannah had her cup of coffee. Another thirty seconds or so, and Michelle had hers. And then Danielle made her cup of tea.

"You look too serious for a social visit," Danielle said as she sat down. "Is this about Phyllis Bates?"

"Yes," Hannah answered.

"And you're investigating?"

"That's right. I have to find the killer, Danielle. Lisa is a suspect and it's the only way I can clear her."

"She doesn't have an alibi?"

"No. We were together until nine at The Cookie Jar, but then she drove home to feed her dogs and let them run in the yard, and I went straight out to The Corner Tavern. She didn't meet me there until around ten."

Danielle looked concerned. "So there was an hour, from nine to ten, when Lisa was alone?"

"That's right."

"And the time of death was . . . ?"

"Between eight and ten," Michelle answered her. "Hannah and I looked at the autopsy report."

Danielle shivered slightly. "I get a sick feeling in my stomach every time I think of that."

Hannah wasn't sure whether Danielle was referring to the autopsy, the fact that Phyllis was murdered, or if it had reminded Danielle of her own husband's violent death. Instead of asking a question that might be painful for Danielle, Hannah decided to change the subject, but Michelle spoke up before Hannah could open her mouth.

"Unfortunately, Lisa *does* have a motive," Michelle said.

"Because Herb dated Phyllis in high school, and now they're working together?" Danielle asked, looking a bit skeptical.

"That's part of it, but there's more," Hannah said. "Mayor Bascomb appointed Phyllis as this year's Mrs. Santa Claus."

Danielle nodded. "I know about that. The

mother of one of my ballet students told me. And she said that Lisa was hoping to be Mrs. Claus."

"That's right," Hannah agreed. "Lisa and I went to the auditorium last night to pick up this year's Christmas gift bags. The Lake Eden Players were just rehearsing the end of *A Christmas Carol,* and we stayed because Lisa wanted to see how Herb and Phyllis would act when they played Mr. and Mrs. Claus."

"Herb with Phyllis," Danielle said with a nod. "That must have been hard for Lisa to take."

"Oh, it's not just that!" Hannah told her. "Usually Santa hugs Mrs. Claus when they've given out candy and cookies to the kids in the audience."

"Yes," Danielle said. "They always do that."

"Well, this year Tory Bascomb decided to do things differently. When she was through criticizing the Mrs. Santa costume that Phyllis was wearing . . ."

"Wait a minute," Danielle interrupted. "Isn't it the same costume that every Mrs. Claus wears?"

"It's supposed to be, but Phyllis claimed that the costume didn't fit and she rented her own costume from a place in the Cities.

Tory said it looked like something a stripper would wear for a routine at Christmas."

Danielle gave a little laugh. "That figures. Was Tory right?"

"Oh, yes. The costume was very revealing."

"And that bothered Lisa?"

"That's only part of it. Tory directed Phyllis to give Herb a stage kiss right before they pulled the final curtain. But Phyllis didn't give him a *stage* kiss. It was a real kiss, and it was obvious that she was interested in Herb."

"Uh-oh," Danielle said. "That must have made Lisa very jealous."

"It did," Michelle told her. "And Herb's been out late almost every night this month. He says he's working late, but Lisa's not so sure that's the truth."

Danielle nodded. "I get it. Working late at the office, hmmm? Do you know that there used to be a bar in St. Cloud called The Office? That way, the guys who came there to drink could say that they were at the office and they wouldn't be lying."

"That's funny, but not really," Michelle said.

"I know." Danielle took a sip of her tea. "Poor Lisa! What can I do to help you, Hannah?"

"Give me a timeline for the drinks you had with the mayor and Stephanie last night."

"I can do that, but . . ." Danielle stopped speaking and her eyes narrowed. "I do understand. The mayor's a suspect because . . . well, you know why. And Stephanie's a suspect because she's always jealous of the women the mayor finds attractive."

"That's right," Hannah said.

"Let me think." Danielle shut her eyes for a moment or two, and then she opened them again. "The mayor and Stephanie picked me up at nine. And Del was already in their car. He told me he'd ridden over to their house to pick up Stephanie. I was watching out the window for them to pull up, and I looked at the clock in the reception area on the way out the door. And we got home at . . . oh, dear. I'm not sure that I even noticed what time. . . ." Danielle stopped speaking and began to smile. "Wait a minute. I can give you the exact time that I got back here."

As Hannah and Michelle watched, Danielle pulled out her cell phone and touched the screen. She touched it a second time and then she nodded. "Ten twenty-five," she told them. "I know because I sent a text to Benton to tell him that I was back so that he could come over when he finished work. The time's right here on the text."

"That clears the mayor," Hannah said.

Danielle looked slightly puzzled. "But it doesn't clear Stephanie?" she asked.

"No. I know that the mayor was in a city council meeting and he left with Del. That means he was with someone for the entire period between eight and ten. But Stephanie wasn't at the city council meeting. She was at home, alone. She had a whole hour, between eight and nine, to drive out to the Corner Tavern and kill Phyllis."

CHOCOLATE CARAMELS
(KATHY & JOHN'S YUMMY NUMMY
CARAMELS FOR MUMMY)

To make this candy, you will need a candy thermometer. I use the kind with a glass tube and a sliding metal clamp that attaches to the side of a saucepan. And even though the recipe calls for a 3-quart saucepan, I always use my 4-quart saucepan. That way I don't have to worry about the candy boiling up over the sides.

1/2 cup finely chopped nuts (*I used walnuts*)

1 cup brown sugar (*pack it down in the cup when you measure it*)

1/2 teaspoon salt

1 cup dark Karo syrup

1 can (*14 ounces*) sweetened condensed milk (*NOT evaporated milk*)

2 ounces unsweetened baking chocolate (*I used Baker's*)

1/2 cup butter (*1 stick, 4 ounces, 1/4 pound*)

1 teaspoon vanilla extract

Before you start, spray a 9-inch by 13-inch cake pan with Pam or another nonstick cooking spray.

Sprinkle the chopped nuts evenly across the bottom of the cake pan.

Place the cake pan on a folded kitchen towel on the kitchen counter.

Get out a 3-quart saucepan (**or a 4-quart saucepan**) and your candy thermometer. Place the thermometer inside the saucepan with the sliding clamp on the outside. Slide the thermometer through the clamp until it's approximately 1/2 inch from the bottom of the saucepan. (**If the bulb touches the bottom of the saucepan, your reading will be wildly off.**)

On a cold burner, combine the brown sugar, salt, dark Karo syrup, sweetened condensed milk, unsweetened chocolate, and butter.

Turn the burner on MEDIUM HIGH heat. STIR the candy mixture CONSTANTLY until it boils. (**This will take about 10 minutes, so pull up a stool and get comfortable while you stir.**)

Continue stirring until your candy thermometer reaches 250 degrees F. Continue to stir for one more minute and move the saucepan to a cold burner.

Add the vanilla extract to the candy mixture and stir it in. (**This could sputter a bit, so be careful.**)

Let the candy mixture sit on the cold

burner for 5 minutes.

When 5 minutes have passed, pour the candy mixture evenly over the nuts in the cake pan. (**Use a heat-resistant spatula so that you can get every delicious drop.**)

Leave the cake pan on the counter for 20 additional minutes to cool. Then cover it with plastic wrap and put it in the refrigerator for at least 3 hours. (**Overnight is fine too.**)

When you're ready to serve your Chocolate Caramels, cut the caramels into squares with a buttered knife. Make sure you cut all the way to the bottom of the cake pan.

Pry out the caramels, one by one, and wrap each one in wax paper.

Yield: 3 dozen or so bonbon-size pieces of delicious candy, depending on the size of the pieces you cut. Store in a covered container.

CHAPTER NINE

"The kitchen smells wonderful!" Michelle said as Hannah pulled the last pan of Chocolate-Covered Mint Cookies from the oven.

"I know. I love to make these cookies. It always reminds me of Christmas. There's something about mint and candy canes that just goes with the whole season."

"And chocolate. Don't forget the chocolate."

"Chocolate's not seasonal. It's good any time of the year. Chocolate's like oxygen. It's elemental."

"You've got a point," Michelle said as she plucked a hot cookie from the baker's rack and juggled it from hand to hand. "Do you think these are too hot to eat?"

"Here." Hannah handed her sister a napkin. "You'd better let it cool a little or you might burn your mouth."

"I've got a better idea. I'll open the door,

stand just inside, and stick out my hand with the cookie. It'll cool faster that way." Michelle opened the back kitchen door, extended her hand, and gasped as a shape materialized from the blowing snow and plucked the cookie from her hand.

"Thanks!" the shape said, stepping closer. "It's not every day that someone comes out to greet me with a hot cookie."

"Mike!" Michelle exclaimed as she recognized him. "You scared me half to death! Give me back that cookie. It's mine."

"Not anymore," Mike said, biting into the cookie as he stepped into the kitchen. "This cookie's too young to be outside alone in weather like this. It's my duty to save it from the storm."

"You ate my cookie!" Michelle accused as Mike popped the rest of the cookie in his mouth.

"There's more where that came from," Hannah said with a laugh. "Sit down, Mike. I'll pour a cup of coffee for you."

Michelle walked over to the baker's rack and piled several more cookies on a napkin. "I'm not taking any more chances with these cookies. I'm going out front to eat them."

Hannah delivered Mike's coffee and dished up a plate of cookies for him. Then she sat down across from him at the workstation. "I figured you'd be here before closing," she said. "You always come around the day after a murder to find out if I've discovered anything."

"These are really good cookies, Hannah." Mike picked one up and took a bite. "Have you?"

Hannah knew exactly what he was asking, but she didn't get up to retrieve her murder book. "Not much."

"But you *are* investigating."

There were times when Hannah wished that Mike didn't know her quite as well as he did. "I'm asking questions if that's what you mean."

"You probably already know that I'll need to talk to Lisa."

"I know. And Lisa knows, too. She mentioned it to me this morning."

"Do you have her name on your suspect list?"

Hannah sighed deeply. "Yes," she admitted. "Lisa's name is there. But I intend to find an alibi for her."

"Any luck so far?"

"Not yet."

They sat there in silence for a moment, and then Hannah sighed again. "Is Herb one of your suspects?"

"Not anymore."

"Why isn't he?" Hannah was certain that she looked just as shocked as she felt.

"Herb has an alibi."

"Wonderful!" Hannah began to smile. "That's a big relief! Does Lisa know that Herb has an alibi?"

Mike shrugged. "I don't know, but I doubt it."

"Can I tell Lisa that you cleared Herb?"

"Sure, you can."

"Good! She'll be really happy to hear that Herb's got an alibi. What is it?"

"Sorry, Hannah. I can't tell you that."

Hannah began to frown. "Why not?"

"Because I promised Herb that I wouldn't tell anyone. And I don't break my promises."

Hannah's frown deepened. "Will Herb tell Lisa his alibi?"

"I'm sure he won't."

Hannah swallowed hard. "Please tell me that Herb's alibi doesn't involve a girl-friend."

"I can do that. Herb's alibi doesn't involve a girlfriend."

"Are you sure? I mean, he's been telling Lisa that he's working late and she's driven past city hall. Herb's not at his office and his car is gone. She's worried that he's spending time with another woman."

"He's not."

"Are you sure?"

"I'm positive." Mike reached out to take Hannah's hand. "Stop worrying, Hannah. And try to get Lisa to stop worrying. Herb isn't with another woman."

"Then where is he until after midnight almost every night?"

"That's privileged information between Herb and me. I can't tell you, Hannah. Now just let it go, okay?"

Hannah didn't like it one little bit, but she nodded. "Okay. I won't ask you any more questions about that. But now that Herb is cleared, who's left on your suspect list?"

Mike laughed. "I knew you'd get around to that, but I just gave you a piece of information. It's your turn to cough up something for me. Who's on *your* suspect list?"

"Mayor Bascomb, but I cleared him."

Mike reached out to tip her chin up so that he could look into her eyes. "Do I detect a slightly disappointed look on your face?"

"Maybe. He *did* have a perfect motive."

"I know. And I cleared him, too. But I asked you who was *on* your list, not who you cleared."

Hannah sighed. She wished that Mike

wasn't quite so logical. She had to give him something before he'd divulge any more information."

"Give it up, Hannah," Mike prompted her.

There was no choice. Hannah knew that she had to tell him. "All right. You win. It's Stephanie Bascomb."

"Stephanie?"

"Yes."

"But she got what she wanted from the mayor. I talked to Claire, and the clothes she bought cost a lot of money. And then I went out to the mall and talked to her jeweler. The mayor paid a small fortune for that ring. Stephanie got her usual revenge and then some."

"I know. I heard about the diamond. Lisa saw it and she said it was as big as a boulder."

"Well . . . Lisa's exaggerating a bit, but it *is* extremely large. But Stephanie already had her new clothes and her new diamond when the victim was murdered. What motive would Stephanie have for actually killing Phyllis?"

"I don't know. Maybe Stephanie thought that Phyllis would do it all over again. Or . . . maybe she wanted to get even with Phyllis for asking the mayor to set her up in an apartment."

"That's weak, Hannah."

"Okay, try this one on for size. Stephanie always supports the Lake Eden Players. She even introduces the actors when they take their curtain call. Maybe she didn't want Phyllis to be Mrs. Claus because she felt that Phyllis wasn't worthy of being included in a Lake Eden Players production."

"That's a little more plausible, but Stephanie has an alibi. She went out for drinks with the mayor after his council meeting."

"Yes, but he didn't pick her up until nine. She was alone before that. And Doc set the window for the time of death from *eight* to ten that night."

"How do you know that?"

"A little birdie told me."

Mike smiled. "A little birdie named Mother?"

"Whatever. I don't have to reveal my sources unless it interferes with your official investigation. We have a deal, don't we?"

"We do."

"If Phyllis was murdered at the beginning of the window of death period, Stephanie would have had time to kill her."

"You think that Stephanie had time to drive out to the Corner Tavern, bash in the victim's head, get rid of the murder weapon, drive back home, clean up, and be dressed and ready to go when the mayor picked her up at nine last night?"

"Yes. It would be tight, but if she was determined to get rid of Phyllis, she could do it. And there's even another possibility that would have saved Stephanie some time. She could have been in the school parking lot, waiting for Phyllis to come out of the auditorium. Rod published the rehearsal schedule in the *Lake Eden Journal.* Stephanie could have followed Phyllis out to the Corner Tavern and intercepted her before she could get inside. That would explain why Bonnie Surma didn't see Phyllis walk in. Stephanie killed Phyllis before she got anywhere near the entrance to the restaurant."

Mike thought about that for a few moments. "It's unlikely, but possible," he conceded. "You were there at the school, Hannah. Did you see Phyllis come out?"

"No. I told you this before. Lisa left before Tory Bascomb dismissed the cast and the crew. When we drove off, none of them had come out yet."

"Did you see Stephanie's car in the school parking lot?"

"No, but there were a lot of other cars and I wasn't looking for it."

"Fair enough. I'll have my team go

through Stephanie's car to see if they can find anything."

"How are you going to do that? Are you going to tell Stephanie that she's a suspect?"

"There's no need for that. Don't worry, Hannah. I have a way to get her car so that my guys can go through it, and it won't arouse either Stephanie's or the mayor's suspicions."

"You're going to do something sneaky?"

"Some might call it that. Others would call it brilliant." Mike gave her the devilish grin that always made Hannah's knees turn weak. "What are you doing for dinner tonight?"

Hannah couldn't hide her look of surprise. "Are you inviting me out to dinner when you're in the middle of an investigation?"

"No. I'd like to ask you out to dinner, but I'm on call until this case is solved. I just want to know where you are at all times. I worry about you, Hannah."

"That's really . . ." Hannah paused, trying to come up with the perfect word. "That's really sweet."

"It's not sweet. It's necessary. You're really good at identifying the killer, but that usually gets you into trouble. I just want a little warning, okay? One of these times I might not be around to protect you. And I *do* want to protect you, Hannah. I care about you." Mike reached out for her hand and gave it a squeeze. "I don't want to see anything bad to happen to you."

Hannah's first instinct was to bristle. She wanted to recount the number of times she'd confronted a killer alone and taken the proper action to save herself. She wasn't some kind of delicate tropical flower that had to be kept in a hothouse and cosseted. But Mike did have a point. She'd gotten into trouble a couple of times and Mike had been there. He *had* saved her. There was no denying that. And she had no way of knowing the future. It was possible that a similar situation could happen again.

"Okay," Hannah told him, although it went totally against her fiercely independent nature. "I'll be glad to give you my schedule for the evening, if it'll make you feel any better."

Mike pulled out the small notebook that he always carried in the shirt pocket of his uniform, and unclipped his pen. "Okay," he said. "Shoot."

"Isn't that a rather dangerous thing for a cop to say?" Hannah asked him, unable to resist the joke.

"Not to you. I know you don't keep a gun

in The Cookie Jar. Where will you be, Hannah?"

"I'll be right here until four-thirty. I'm going to let Lisa close up today. Michelle and I will head back to the condo to get something to eat and feed Moishe. And then we'll drive back to town to attend the last rehearsal of the play at the school auditorium."

"And after that?"

"Back to the condo until early tomorrow morning, when Michelle and I should get here about five. You're welcome to drop by then for coffee and cookies if you want to check up on me and get the schedule for my day."

"Thanks, Hannah. I appreciate that. And you won't go anywhere else?"

"I'm not planning on it."

Mike looked properly grateful for her cooperation, and Hannah couldn't help but wonder if they were on a new footing as she walked him to the door. When they got there, she opened it for Mike, but he didn't step out. Instead, he pulled her into his arms and gave her a hug. "If you deviate from the schedule you gave me for tonight, please text or call," Mike told her after ending the hug. "I don't want to remove another cold dead body from a snowbank."

CHOCOLATE-COVERED
MINT COOKIES

Preheat oven to 350 degrees F., rack in the middle position.

1 cup salted butter, softened (*2 sticks, 8 ounces, 1/2 pound*)

1 small package (*makes 4 half-cups*) chocolate instant pudding mix (*NOT sugar-free*)

1/2 cup white (*granulated*) sugar

1/2 cup packed brown sugar

1 egg, beaten

1 teaspoon vanilla extract

1 teaspoon baking soda

1/4 teaspoon salt

1/2 teaspoon ground cinnamon

1 and 1/2 cups all-purpose flour (*pack it down in the cup when you measure it*)

1 and 1/2 cups quick rolled oats (*not instant — the Quick 1-minute kind*)

1 cup chocolate-covered mints (*I used Junior Mints*)

1 cup semi-sweet chocolate chips (*a 6-ounce package — I used Nestle*)

In a medium bowl and using an electric mixer, on MEDIUM SPEED, beat the softened butter with the dry chocolate pudding mix. Beat until the mixture is light and fluffy.

Add the white sugar and the brown sugar. Continue to beat on **MEDIUM** speed until the contents are well-mixed.

Add the egg and the vanilla. Mix well.

Add the baking soda, salt, and cinnamon. Mix until they are well incorporated.

Add the flour in half-cup increments, mixing after each addition.

Add the rolled oats in half-cup increments, mixing after each addition.

Remove the bowl from the mixer and give it a final stir by hand. You will finish the rest of this recipe by hand.

Stir in the chocolate-covered mints by hand, being careful not to over-stir and crush them.

Add the semi-sweet chocolate chips and stir them in. Again, stir lightly so that you don't crush the mints.

Prepare your cookie sheets by lining them with parchment paper, or spraying lightly with Pam or another non-stick cooking spray.

Drop, by rounded teaspoons, no more than 12 cookies to a standard-sized sheet. You can also use a 2-teaspoon size scooper if you wish.

Bake the Chocolate-Covered Mint Cookies at 350 degrees F. for 10 to 12 minutes or until the edges are golden brown.

Cool the cookies for 2 minutes on the cookie sheet, and then remove them to a wire rack to complete cooling. (*If you've used parchment paper, you can simply leave the cookies on the paper and pull it over to the wire rack.*) Wait until the cookies are completely cool before you try to peel them off the parchment paper.

Yield: Makes approximately 5 dozen deliciously minty and chocolatey cookies.

CHAPTER TEN

"Thanks, Norman!" Hannah said, as Norman walked in the door of the Jordan High auditorium carrying a very large box. She knew exactly what was in the box because she'd called him earlier and asked him to bring his popcorn machine to the auditorium.

"No problem. I've got all the things you need to make a batch of popcorn in the car. I'll go get the other box."

Hannah quickly shrugged into her parka. "Hold on a second and I'll walk out with you."

"Okay, but I don't need help. Wouldn't you rather stay here, where it's warm?"

"No, I'd rather go with you. Come on, Norman. Let's get that second box so we can figure out how to use your popcorn machine before it's time for the first intermission."

"But there's no audience. It's just a rehearsal."

"I know, but the Lake Eden Players might like some popcorn to munch on between acts. And everyone on the makeup and technical crews would enjoy it."

"You're right, Hannah. Let's go."

Norman led the way outside and Hannah followed. The moment they got outside the door, Norman turned to her. "Okay, Hannah. Why did you need to talk to me alone?"

Hannah smiled. She should have known that Norman would catch her true purpose in walking out with him. "Because Lisa was standing with Michelle at the counter and I wanted to ask you if you'd discovered anything that might help to clear her."

"Makes sense. And, as a matter of fact, I did discover a partial alibi for her."

"Oh, Norman! You're wonderful!" Hannah threw her arms around him and gave him a hug. It wasn't much of a hug because they were both wearing bulky, padded parkas and her arms barely reached around him. "Tell me what you discovered."

"I stopped by Mother and Earl's this afternoon. Earl was there, warming up after a whole morning of plowing out Lake Eden city streets, and Mother was making Janelle's Chicken Soup for him."

"I love that soup! I wish I'd gone with you."

"So do I. You know I love to spend time with you, Hannah. Anyway, I had a bowl of soup with them, and Earl and I got to talking. Earl said he was driving the snowplow last night."

"Last night," Hannah repeated, beginning to understand why Norman was telling her about Earl's snowplow schedule. "Where did Earl plow? And when?"

"That's what I love about you Hannah." Norman slipped his arm around her waist as they walked to his car. "You catch on right away."

"Maybe. What time?"

"He was going to plow Lisa's street at nine-thirty-five, but he noticed that Lisa's car was parked in front of the house. He knows that Lisa and Herb have a two-car garage and they always park there when they come home at night. Since Lisa's car was out on the street, Earl figured that she planned to go out again."

"That was smart of him," Hannah commented.

"I thought so, too. Earl told me that the plow he uses leaves a pretty high bank of snow and he didn't want to block Lisa in if she needed to get her car out again, so he passed by her street and started plowing a few streets over."

"Earl's a really nice guy," Hannah said, having trouble containing her excitement. "When did he come back with the plow?"

"He thinks it was about ten minutes later because he plowed the streets on either side of her."

"And when Earl got back there, Lisa's car was gone?"

"Yes. That helps, doesn't it, Hannah?"

"Yes! It proves that Lisa went home to feed the dogs. And it takes fifteen minutes to get from Lisa's house to the Corner Tavern."

"That means Lisa couldn't have gotten there until ten minutes before ten. And then there's only another ten minutes of her time that's unaccounted for?"

"That's right. It doesn't clear Lisa, but it makes her a much more unlikely suspect. Lisa met me inside at around ten. And that means she would have had only ten minutes to kill Phyllis, change to her ankle boots, and hurry into the restaurant to meet me." Hannah put her arms around Norman again and hugged him as tightly as she could. "Thank you so much! It helps a whole lot."

"Does it help enough to invite me to your

place after the rehearsal is over?"

"Of course it does!" Hannah responded immediately. "You know you're always welcome."

"Good. I'll stop for pizza and meet you and Michelle at the condo. And now, we'd better get these supplies inside before the first act ends and we don't have time to figure out the machine and make the popcorn."

"That went well!" Hannah commented as she drove out of the school parking lot and headed for the highway.

"And everyone loved the popcorn," Michelle reported. "There were quite a few people who came straight from work and they were really hungry."

"I'm going to drive past The Cookie Jar to make sure our Christmas lights are on," Hannah told her. "I had to move the timer this morning, and I'm not sure I set the time correctly."

"Why did you have to move it?"

"Lisa told me that one of our customers almost tripped over the extension cord, so I decided to move the timer to a closer wall socket."

"That was probably smart."

"While I was at it, I put on a new timer,

183

too. It's one that fits flat to the wall with the plug on the side." Hannah drove up to Main Street and turned at the corner. The lights were on, and she gave a satisfied smile as they went past. "I must have done it right. They're still on."

"And they look really good. I'm glad that all the businesses on Main Street leave their Christmas lights on at night."

"So am I. It really looks festive. Herb was smart convincing everyone that leaving on the Christmas lights was a deterrent to thieves."

"Speaking of Herb, did you manage to talk to Lisa?"

"Yes." Hannah turned onto the highway and drove toward her condo complex. "I think I convinced her that Herb isn't seeing another woman. I told her exactly what Mike told me, and that seemed to satisfy her. And she was very relieved that Herb had an alibi."

"Do you mind if I bake when we get to your place? It won't take long."

"I never mind when you bake. What are you making?"

"A Christmas Orange Raisin Cake."

"Is that a new recipe?"

"Not really. It's an adaptation of Grandma Elsa's Christmas Date Cake. I've been thinking about it all day, and I've got everything I need to make it."

There was very little traffic, and it didn't take long to drive to the condo complex, and Hannah parked in her designated spot in the underground garage. The two sisters walked up the outside staircase together, and Hannah gave a little wave as she spotted Moishe on the window ledge, waiting for them to get home. "I guess it's a little silly to wave to Moishe," she said with a laugh. "You're not going to believe this, but once he waved back at me."

"You're kidding, aren't you?" Michelle asked.

"No. When I climbed up the stairs and waved at him, he raised his right paw and put it up against the glass."

"Okay," Michelle said, but she didn't sound convinced. "Maybe he was after a bug or something."

"Maybe, but I prefer to believe that he was waving back at me." Hannah reached the landing first and waited for Michelle to climb the last few steps. "You, or me?" she asked.

"I'll do it." Michelle positioned herself for the furry orange and white ball that would jump through the air and land in her arms once the door was opened.

"Ready?" Hannah asked her.

"Ready."

Hannah unlocked the door and stood to the side. She reached out to open it, moved out of the way just in time, and watched as Moishe hurtled himself airborne and straight into Michelle's waiting arms.

"Oooofff!" Michelle said, and it was a cross between a laugh and a groan. "I always forget how heavy he is."

"Twenty-three pounds and counting," Hannah said as Michelle walked inside, placed Moishe on the back of the couch, and hurried into the kitchen to get the fish-shaped, salmon-flavored treats he loved.

"Here you go, Moishe," Michelle said, coming back with the cannister and placing three kitty treats in front of Moishe. "When Norman brings pizza and gives you sausage, you could gain another half-pound or so before the night is over."

CHRISTMAS ORANGE RAISIN CAKE

Preheat oven to 325 degrees F., rack in the middle position

Hannah's 1st Note: Michelle modified this recipe and Norman loves it. He wants me to make it for him every Christmas.

The Fruit:

2 cups golden raisins (*you can also use regular raisins, but Norman prefers golden raisins*)

2 cups boiling water

2 teaspoons baking soda

1/2 cup triple sec or Grand Marnier (*substitute orange juice if you don't want to use alcohol*)

1/2 cup orange juice

Mother, who's always frugal and absolutely doesn't have to be, says to tell you that triple sec is a lot cheaper than Grand Marnier.

Place the raisins in a bowl. Pour the boiling water over the golden raisins, add the baking soda (*it foams up a bit*) and then add the liqueur and orange juice.

Set the raisins and liquid aside on the kitchen counter to cool.

While the raisins are cooling, place the

following ingredients together in another large mixing bowl or in the bowl of an electric mixer:

The Cake Batter:
1 cup softened salted butter (**2 sticks, 8 ounces, 2 1/2 pound**)
2 cups white (**granulated**) sugar
4 large eggs
1/2 teaspoon salt
1 Tablespoon orange zest (**That's finely grated orange peel, but just the orange part, not the white under it.**)
3 cups all-purpose flour (**don't sift — pack it down in the cup when you measure it**)

Turn the mixer to MEDIUM speed and mix thoroughly, or beat thoroughly by hand.

Take a raisin out of your first bowl to see if it's plumped. If it's round and looks as if it's absorbed liquid, add the raisins AND the liquid to the mixing bowl.

Mix your cake batter thoroughly on MEDIUM speed or by hand until everything has been thoroughly incorporated.

Butter and flour a 9-inch by 13-inch rectangular cake pan. You can also spray the inside of the cake pan with Pam for baking (**the kind of Pam with flour in it**).

Hannah's 2nd Note: This cake rises

about an inch and a half, so make sure the sides of your cake pan are tall enough.

Pour the cake batter into the pan. Then sprinkle the following on the top, in this order, BEFORE baking:

Cake Topping:

12 ounces milk chocolate chips (*2 cups*)

1 cup white (*granulated*) sugar

1 cup chopped pecans (*you can use any nuts you like — Norman prefers walnuts — I prefer pecans*)

Bake your cake at 325 degrees F. for 80 minutes, or until you test it and it's done.

Testing Your Cake for Doneness:

Use a long toothpick or a cake tester to tell if your cake is done. If you insert it one inch from the center of the cake, it should come out clean without batter sticking to it. If it doesn't, bake your cake in additional 5-minute increments until your tester comes out clean. Remove the cake from the oven.

Hannah's 3rd Note: If you happen to stick the toothpick in and hit a chocolate chip, it'll come out covered with melted chocolate — just wipe it off and stick it in again to test the actual cake batter.

Let the cake cool in the pan on a wire rack or a cold stove burner. It can be served slightly warm, at room temperature, or chilled.

Hannah's 4th Note: If you want to be fancy, cut this cake into pieces, put it on dessert plates, and top each piece with a dollop of sweetened whipped cream. Then garnish the whipped cream with chocolate shavings or chocolate curls scraped from a milk chocolate candy bar. Alternatively, if you don't want to use chocolate, you can top each slice with a dollop of sweetened whipped cream and put a red maraschino cherry on top.

CHAPTER ELEVEN

Hannah wasn't sure what had awakened her. Perhaps it was the bluish-white light that had begun to glow at the foot of her bed, turning the dark night into something foreign, something unknown.

"Dad?" she asked, sitting up in bed.

"I'm here, Honey-bear. Or at least I'm almost here. Give me a minute to pull myself together, okay?"

Hannah wanted to laugh, but she was too amazed to do anything but stare. Her father *was* pulling himself together, right before her very eyes. The bluish-white cloud was forming itself into an oval. Once the oval was roughly her father's height, appendages began to grow, four of them in the proper places for arms and legs. The head was next, popping up from the top of the oval like a balloon on a string being jerked from above.

"Almost there," the head said in her father's voice. "They let me come to visit

191

you again. I'm playing the Ghost of Christmas Present tonight. And all I have to do for the favor is to barbecue for the AITs next week."

"The AITs?"

"Angels in training. It hasn't been that long since they were human, and they still get hungry. We're having bratwurst and beans."

Hannah smiled. "That was your favorite meal to make for us when Mother was gone."

"That was because it was easy. Throw the sausage on the grill and heat a can of beans."

"But all of us loved it. We loved your chicken, beef, turkey noodle soup, too."

"Three cans of soup thrown in a pot and heated together. It was easy, too. It's not like I made the soup from scratch."

"But that's okay. It was good and we always had it with oyster crackers. All three of us loved the fact that you cared enough to cook for us."

"Of course I did. I still do. You never lose the love, Hannah. It survives forever."

Hannah blinked back the tears that had formed in her eyes. It was wonderful to know that her dad still loved her.

"Uh-oh. They just called me. It's time for

your peek into the present, Hannah. Watch this."

As Hannah watched, the movie screen materialized and images appeared. It was morning in Lake Eden and she was walking down the street toward Florence's Red Owl Grocery. She didn't go inside the grocery store. She stopped by the door to Danielle's dance studio. There was a pretty wreath hanging on the inside of the glass door, and Hannah took a moment to admire it. Then she opened the door and began to climb the long, carpeted staircase.

The scene shifted to the reception area, and Hannah found herself sitting there, waiting for Danielle to finish with her class. Then Danielle came out and the scene shifted again to Danielle's tiny kitchen, the same kitchen Hannah and Michelle had visited less than twenty-four hours ago. This time, Michelle wasn't there. And then Hannah was leaving, going down the carpeted stairs. She stopped at the door to the street, pulled out her murder book and turned to the suspect page. She took a moment to jot down a name.

"That's all," her father said and Hannah squinted, trying to read the name that was still faintly visible on the screen, but the screen went blank before she could decipher the letters. Her glimpse into the present was over.

"Remember, Hannah. You must remember this tomorrow. It's very important."

"Yes, Dad. I'll try to remember. Really, I will."

"I know. I love you, Honey-bear. I'm hoping they'll let me come back one final time to visit you. Until then . . ."

Hannah watched as her father's shape flickered and morphed into the bluish-white cloud again. The cloud moved, closer, closer, and then it surrounded her and she felt a kiss on her forehead. "Dad," she whispered, tears rolling down her cheeks. "Don't go, Dad! Please!"

"I must, Honey-bear. They're calling me. Just try to remember . . . remember . . . remember . . ."

"Remember," Hannah repeated, reaching out toward him and encountering nothing but empty air. And then her eyelids closed. And she slept a deep and dreamless sleep.

Someone with very rough lips was kissing her cheek. It was not completely unpleasant, but it was a bit disconcerting. Hannah opened her eyes to see Moishe staring down at her with his one good eye and purring.

"Good heavens!" she exclaimed, sitting

194

up quickly. "What time is it?"

Of course Moishe did not answer, but one glance at her bedside alarm clock confirmed that she had, indeed, slept in. It was almost five in the morning and she normally got up at four-thirty. Hannah felt around for her slippers, located them under the side of the bed, and slipped them on her feet. Then she shrugged into her robe and sniffed the air.

"Coffee," she told Moishe with a smile. "And . . . something with raspberries?"

"Rrrroww!" Moishe concurred.

"Let's go see what it is." Hannah hurried down the carpeted hallway with Moishe trailing a bit behind her, swatting at the ties of her robe hanging down either side because she hadn't bothered to secure them around her waist.

"Great!" Michelle said as Hannah and Moishe entered the kitchen. "Now I won't have to wake you."

"Moishe took care of that. He licked my face to wake me up."

"That's probably because he was in a hurry for his breakfast. He knows I always give him something special when I stay with you."

Michelle scooped kitty crunchies into Moishe's bowl, followed by something from the frying pan.

"Shrimp?" Hannah guessed.

"No. I cut up a little piece of leftover chicken and warmed it on the stove."

"No wonder he's always so glad to see you!" Hannah exclaimed. And then she smiled. "Actually, both of us are. I smelled the coffee."

Michelle gestured toward Hannah's kitchen table and came over with the mug she'd just filled. "Here you go."

Hannah took a big sip and gave a grateful sigh. "Thanks. I really needed this. You made something else too, and it smells delicious. Does it have raspberries?"

"Yes. I baked Red Raspberry Muffins. I wanted something with fruit, and you had some frozen raspberries. The muffins should be cool enough if you want to try one now."

"Yes!" Hannah said emphatically. "You always make really good muffins, Michelle."

"Thanks. This one's an experiment. Let me know if you can think of any improvements."

Hannah accepted a muffin from Michelle, peeled off the double cupcake papers, and took a bite without even bothering to break it apart and butter it."

"Mmmmmmm!" she said, taking another bite just to be sure. "No improvements are

196

necessary. These are perfect, just the way they are."

The two sisters ate in silence for several minutes, and then Hannah got up to pour more coffee for both of them. When she came back, she was frowning slightly.

"What is it?' Michelle asked, noticing Hannah's frown.

"I'm not sure. There's something niggling at the back of my mind."

"Niggling." Michelle looked pensive. "You use that word all the time. Is that like jiggling and nudging at the same time?"

"That's exactly what it is! This time it's a feeling that I should go to see Danielle again. But I don't understand why. We found out everything we needed to know from her . . . didn't we?"

"I thought so, but I don't know for sure. Were you thinking that Danielle might know something more about Phyllis's murder?"

"Maybe. Were you in school when Boyd Watson was hired, Michelle?"

"Yes, except he wasn't the head coach. And I don't think he was married to Danielle yet. They were just dating, and she used to come to all of his games. I know she wasn't from Lake Eden because nobody at school knew her. And I think she was younger than Coach Watson was."

"And was that when Phyllis was a cheer-leader?"

"I don't think so, but I'm not positive. Maybe you should ask Danielle."

"I think I will." Hannah was about to break her muffin apart and butter it when she felt a strange sensation. She dropped it back on her plate and put her hand to her cheek.

"Do you have a toothache?" Michelle asked her.

"No. No, I don't. Everything's fine, Michelle." Hannah was smiling as she picked up her muffin again and began to butter it. Michelle would probably have her locked up in a padded room if she admitted she believed that their dad had been with her for an instant, just long enough to give her a kiss on the cheek!

At precisely nine o'clock, Hannah walked down Main Street with a bag of Red Raspberry Muffins in her hand, headed for Danielle's dance studio. She'd remembered even more about her strange dream, or whatever it was, and today was eerily similar to the one her father had shown on the movie screen. As Hannah neared the dance studio, she wondered what would happen if she walked on past the glass door. Would her father somehow push her back and guide her to where he wanted her to go?

Even though she was curious about what would happen, Hannah stopped at Danielle's door when she noticed the Christmas wreath that decorated the inside of the glass. It hadn't been there when she'd visited Danielle yesterday, but it was there now. And it was exactly the same as the wreath that her father had shown her.

Hannah felt an eerie sense of being directed as she climbed up the stairs, entered the reception area, and took a chair to wait for Danielle's class to end. She shivered slightly as she realized that everything was exactly the same as the scenes that her father had shown her. The implication was too much for her rational mind to handle, but she was here and she needed to talk to Danielle. Perhaps it was a coincidence. Perhaps it was due to her curious mind working overtime in her sleep. Or perhaps all this was something her mind refused to process. All she knew for certain was that she should forget about everything else and concentrate on how to get the answers she needed from Danielle.

RED RASPBERRY MUFFINS

Preheat oven to 375 degrees F., rack in the middle position.

Muffin Batter:

3/4 cup (*1 and 1/2 sticks, 6 ounces*) salted butter

1 cup white (*granulated*) sugar

2 beaten eggs (*just whip them up in a glass with a fork*)

2 teaspoons baking powder

1/2 teaspoon cinnamon

1/2 teaspoon salt

2 and 1/4 cups all-purpose flour (*pack it down in the cup when you measure it*)

1/2 cup whole milk

1/2 cup seedless raspberry jam

1 cup fresh OR frozen raspberries

Crumb Topping:

1/2 cup white (*granulated*) sugar

1/2 teaspoon cinnamon

1/3 cup all-purpose flour (*pack it down in the cup when you measure it*)

1/4 cup (*1/2 stick, 2 ounces*) salted butter, softened

Grease the bottoms only of a 12-cup muffin pan (*or line the cups with double cupcake papers — that's what I do at The*

***Cookie Jar*)**

Melt the butter in a bowl or measuring cup in the microwave. (***This takes me about a minute in the microwave on HIGH.***)

Set the melted butter on the kitchen counter to cool.

Measure out the sugar in a large bowl.

Mix in the beaten eggs.

Add the baking powder, cinnamon, and salt. Mix thoroughly.

Cup your hands around the bowl containing the melted butter. If it's cool enough so it won't cook the eggs, stir it into your mixing bowl with the rest of the ingredients.

Add <u>half</u> of the flour to your bowl and mix it in.

Add the whole milk to your bowl and mix that in.

Add the <u>other half</u> of the flour to your bowl and mix until everything is incorporated.

Mix in the half cup of seedless raspberry jam.

If you're using a mixer, take the bowl out of the mixer, scrape down the sides of the bowl, and give the contents a stir with a spoon by hand.

Add the raspberries and mix them in by hand.

Fill the prepared muffin cups three-quarters full and set them aside. If you have muffin batter left over, grease the bottom of a small tea-bread loaf pan and fill it with your remaining batter.

Make the crumb topping by mixing the sugar, cinnamon, and flour in a small bowl with a fork. Add the softened butter and cut it in until it's crumbly. (*You can also do this in a food processor with chilled butter that you've cut into chunks. Use the steel blade in an on-and-off motion until the resulting mixture resembles coarse gravel.*)

Fill the remaining space in the muffin cups with the crumb topping. If you had batter left over and used the tea-bread pan, reserve some topping to sprinkle over that.

Bake the muffins in a 375 F. degree oven for 25 to 30 minutes. (*The tea-bread should bake from 5 to 10 minutes longer than the muffins, but test it with a cake tester or long toothpick when your muffins are done. Insert the tester in the center of the loaf. If your tester comes out clean, your tea-bread is done.*)

When your muffins are baked, take them out of the oven and set the muffin pan on a wire rack or a cold stovetop burner to cool for at least 30 minutes. (*The muffins need to cool in the pan for easy removal.*) Then just tip them out of the cups, or lift them out by the edges of the cupcake papers. Serve with salted butter for those who want it, and enjoy.

These muffins are wonderful when they're slightly warm, but the raspberry flavor will intensify if you store them in a covered container overnight.

Yield: 12 delicious muffins with a little batter left over for several more muffins or a small loaf of tea-bread.

CHAPTER TWELVE

"Do you have a couple of minutes to talk?" Hannah asked, handing the muffins to Danielle.

"Normally, no. I usually have a private class right after the one that just ended, but it's cancelled for today." Danielle looked down at the bag. "Whatever is in here smells divine! What did you bring, Hannah?"

"Red Raspberry Muffins. Michelle made them for breakfast this morning."

"I love raspberries! Let's go in the kitchen. I'll put on the coffee and then we can talk."

Several minutes later, Hannah was seated at Danielle's kitchen table, holding a cup of French roast coffee. "You make good coffee, Danielle."

"It's the coffeemaker and the pods, but thank you. I'm getting better in the kitchen, but I'm afraid I'll never be a really good cook. And I'd never be able to make anything as luscious as these muffins!"

"I'll tell Michelle that you like them."

"Good!" Danielle took another bite and smiled. "Heavenly! Now I'm almost glad that Bonnie cancelled her class this morning."

"Bonnie?"

"Bonnie Surma. She's taking private lessons from me to learn some dance routines that she can use with the Jordan High cheerleaders."

Hannah knew that she must have looked completely puzzled, because Danielle went on to explain.

"Bonnie used to coach the cheerleaders ten years or so ago. That was about the time that you were in high school, wasn't it, Hannah?"

"Yes, it was. But I don't remember that."

"Were you a cheerleader?"

"Heavens, no! Andrea was the one who went to the try-outs, not me. I never was very athletic."

"Then that's probably why you didn't know that Bonnie was coaching the cheerleaders."

"I remember that Bonnie was always at the school for one thing or another. She did a lot of things there, but I never knew that she was involved with the cheerleaders."

"Well, she was. Boyd told me that she had

classes for the cheerleaders in the gym after school on Mondays and Wednesdays. Bonnie was a head cheerleader in college and she taught the girls all the cheers she remembered. It was part of her volunteer work. She's always been very active with the school, and in the community, too."

"I know," Hannah said with a smile. "Bonnie belongs to as many clubs as my mother does. And that's a whole lot!"

"To tell the truth, I don't know how Bonnie does it. She never backs down when they ask her to do something, and she's on the board of almost every charity. She's very active with the children's home, and she even volunteers at the senior center."

Hannah's mind was spinning so fast at this new information, she wasn't quite sure what to ask next. But that didn't matter because Danielle began to elaborate.

"I think that's one of the reasons why Bonnie cancelled her class today. She must be very upset about what happened to Phyllis Bates. Phyllis was one of Bonnie's cheerleaders, and Bonnie worked very hard to turn Phyllis's life around. Bonnie and Gil never had children and Phyllis was like a daughter to Bonnie. She took Phyllis shopping for the right kind of clothes, gave her advice on everything from schoolwork to dating, and picked her up for church every Sunday."

"Bonnie told you all that?"

"Yes. Bonnie's a fascinating woman, a real do-gooder, and I mean that in a positive way. She said that Phyllis was heading down the wrong path when she was in junior high, flirting with the older boys and wearing clothes that were too provocative. Bonnie just knew that Phyllis would get into trouble if she didn't change her ways, so she took Phyllis under her wing."

"By encouraging Phyllis to try out for the junior varsity cheerleading squad?" Hannah guessed.

"That's right. Bonnie said she did her best to teach Phyllis how to be a lady and maintain good grades and good moral values. And Bonnie was proud that her effort had worked. Phyllis gained self-confidence and began to date a really nice senior boy."

"Herb Beeseman," Hannah said.

"Yes. Bonnie said that Herb was a very good influence on Phyllis. Phyllis had never dated such a nice boy before. And then Phyllis's mother moved to Minneapolis, and Bonnie lost touch with Phyllis."

Hannah was beginning to see the whole picture. "And Bonnie didn't know what had happened to Phyllis until Mayor Bascomb hired her and Phyllis moved back here to Lake Eden?"

"Exactly. It just about killed Bonnie when she heard that Phyllis was involved with Mayor Bascomb. She didn't want to believe it at first. Phyllis was Bonnie's big success story, and she was doing everything that Bonnie had taught her not to do."

"Bonnie must have been terribly disappointed in Phyllis."

"Oh, she was. And Bonnie didn't know what she could do about it. She was desolate, Hannah, and horribly depressed. I've known Bonnie for quite a while now, and I've never seen her so upset."

Hannah felt a chill run through her. "Did Bonnie try to talk to Phyllis, to set her back on the right track again?"

"Bonnie was going to do exactly that, but before she had the chance, the mayor broke it off with Phyllis and reassigned her to Herb's office. Bonnie was sure that Herb would have a good influence on Phyllis, now that he was married and all, and everyone in town knew that he was in love with his wife."

Hannah asked the question again, just to be sure. "So Bonnie never talked to Phyllis about her . . . behavior with the mayor?"

"I don't think so. She would have told me if she had. And then the mayor appointed Phyllis as Mrs. Claus, and that changed everything for Bonnie. I talked to her on the phone right after I heard about it, and Bonnie said she thought that playing Mrs. Claus might be a turning point for Phyllis. She said she hoped that playing a sweet, kind woman on stage would have a real positive effect. Bonnie said that we learn by doing and she hoped that Phyllis would learn from the experience."

"I . . . see," Hannah said, scenes from the rehearsal she'd seen flashing through her mind. Phyllis's inappropriate costume, the way she'd kissed Herb, and the fact that Bonnie had been sitting next to Tory Bascomb and watching the whole thing.

"Poor Bonnie!" Danielle said with a sigh. "My heart goes out to her, especially now that she's so sick."

That got Hannah's attention. "Bonnie's sick?" she asked.

"Yes. That's why she cancelled her private lesson today. Bonnie caught a terrible cold and she's running a fever. She's blaming it all on the fact that she has holes in her boots and she got her feet wet in the snow. Bonnie's very frugal and she patched the holes with duct tape, but she admitted that it didn't work very well and she was avoiding deep snow."

"I'm sorry Bonnie's sick," Hannah said, hoping to keep the conversation going.

"So am I. Bonnie told me that it's just a cold, but I think it might be something more serious than that."

"Why do you think that?"

"Because doctors don't usually prescribe antibiotics for a common cold, and Bonnie told me that Doc Knight put her on antibiotics. My guess is that Bonnie got run down worrying about Phyllis and her immune system couldn't fight off the bug she got. Now she's not only sick, she's also grieving for Phyllis because she never got the opportunity to talk to her and try to help her."

Or did she get that opportunity? Hannah's mind asked the question, but this wasn't the time to say it out loud. She'd consider it later, after she was alone and could think clearly.

"Thanks for telling me, Danielle," Hannah said, getting to her feet. "I'll drop in on Bonnie later to bring her some soup or something. Do you know if she's home?"

"I don't know for sure, but I think she probably is. She sounded awful when she called me this morning, and I really doubt that she left the house. When you see her, please give her my best and tell her I said to get well in a hurry."

Hannah was thoughtful as she walked down the long staircase. Her mind was churning with unanswered questions. When she got down to the outside door, she stopped and drew her murder book out of her purse. She turned to the suspects page and was about to write down Bonnie Surma's name when she remembered that she had done the very same thing before.

"Not now," Hannah said out loud. She wouldn't think about her father, and the dreams she'd had, and anything else right now. She jotted down Bonnie's name, thrust her murder book back in her purse, and pulled open the outside door.

Hannah thought about Bonnie and Phyllis all the way back to The Cookie Jar. When she got there, she was glad to see that the kitchen was deserted and everyone was out in front, waiting on customers. She needed time to think. And she needed time to devise a way to get Bonnie to tell her what she knew.

Even though Hannah didn't think that Bonnie had murdered her former protégé, she couldn't dismiss that possibility. The Ghost of Christmas Present had shown her an image of what she'd written in her murder book. She had been unable to read it, but she was fast becoming convinced that it had been Bonnie's name.

Hannah thought back to her first visitation, the one from the Ghost of Christmas Past. Bonnie had been sitting on a stool at the bar in the Corner Tavern when Hannah had walked in. When the stool next to Hannah had become vacant, Bonnie had moved to join her and Hannah had looked over to make sure that Bonnie hadn't left any of her belongings behind.

"Shoes!" Hannah said aloud, remembering that Bonnie had been wearing bright red tennis shoes and gray and orange argyle socks. The socks were Gil's. Hannah was sure of it. Gil Surma had always been fond of argyle socks, and he wore them to school every day. Red shoes with a pair of her husband's gray and orange socks was an odd combination for Bonnie. She was someone who normally dressed conservatively. Bonnie's tennis shoes hadn't looked wet, and there had been no puddles of moisture in the sawdust on the floor. Had Bonnie worn her damaged boots inside the Corner Tavern and changed to her tennis shoes when she'd hung up her coat? And had the only dry socks in her car been a pair of Gil's?

Hannah jotted a note. Where were Bonnie's boots? Were they still on the boot rack at the Corner Tavern? There was only one way to find out, and Hannah was just getting up from her stool at the workstation when Michelle came into the kitchen.

"Hi, Hannah. I didn't hear you come in. Did Danielle like the muffins?"

"She loved them. She was going to save one for Benton, but I'm not placing any bets that he'll actually get it."

Michelle laughed. "Did you find out what you needed to know?"

"I'm not sure. About the only thing I know for sure is that Bonnie Surma is sick. Danielle told me that. I thought it might be nice to take her something to cheer her up. What do we have that might be good for someone who's got a terrible cold?"

"Janelle's Chicken Soup," Michelle answered immediately. "I made a pot the last time I was here at The Cookie Jar, and I stuck some in the freezer. I'll get it out and thaw it for you."

"Perfect. Thanks, Michelle."

"Take some Butterscotch Crunch Fudge, too. Lisa and I made it while you were at Danielle's dance studio. It's in the cooler and it should be ready to cut by now. It's delicious, and Bonne's bound to like that. I'd give you one of the Cashew Candy Rolls we made for the opening night of the play, but they're not hard enough to cut yet."

"That's okay. I'm sure Bonnie will love the soup and the Butterscotch Crunch Candy."

"The recipe for the candy is on the counter. Take it with you if Bonnie wants to know the ingredients. I'll pack everything up for you right now."

"Okay. I'm running out to the Corner Tavern first to check something out. Do you want me to bring some food back for your lunch?"

"Thanks, but no. Lonnie's coming to pick me up and we're going down to Hal and Rose's Café for lunch. I was about to ask you if you wanted to come along."

"I haven't had one of Rose's roast beef sandwiches in ages. How long do you plan to be there?"

"An hour if that's okay with you. That's how long Lonnie has for lunch. And if Mike can get away to join us, it might be a little longer than that."

"An hour's fine with me, and so is longer. Take all the time you want, Michelle. It's not like I'm paying you for working here, or anything. I may drop by on my way back from Bonnie's house if you're still there. I'll give you a call on your cell when I leave Bonnie's."

"Okay, Hannah. Don't forget to stay in touch with Mike. I know he asked you to."

"I won't. And don't worry, Michelle. I'm just going out to the Corner Tavern and over to Bonnie's house. I'll be perfectly fine."

Butterscotch Crunch Candy

You do NOT need a candy thermometer to make this candy.

half of a 15-ounce bag of salted stick pretzels (*the thin stick kind — I used Snyder's*)

14-ounce can of sweetened condensed milk (*I used Eagle Brand — do NOT use evaporated milk*)

1/4 teaspoon salt

2 cups (*12 ounces*) butterscotch chips (*I use Nestle*)

Hannah's 1st Note: you can make this candy in a heavy saucepan on the stove over MEDIUM heat or in a large, microwave-safe bowl in the microwave on HIGH. Either will work just fine.

Put the pretzels into a bowl and break them into pieces. You don't have to be exact, but try to make sure each pretzel is broken into at least 4 pieces.

Hannah's 2nd Note: When Lisa and I make this candy at The Cookie Jar, we put the pretzels in a large, sealable, plastic bag and crush them up with a rolling pin until there are no large pieces left.

Prepare an 8-inch square brownie pan by

lining it with a piece of heavy-duty foil that is large enough to stick up at least two inches above the sides of your pan. You will use these "ears" of foil to lift out your candy after it has cooled and hardened.

Spray the inside of the foil with Pam or another non-stick cooking spray.

Open the can of sweetened, condensed milk and pour it into another microwave-safe bowl.

Sprinkle the salt on top of the sweetened condensed milk.

Place the 2 cups of butterscotch chips on the top.

Stir everything up with a heat-resistant rubber spatula.

Set aside your spatula and microwave the contents of the bowl on HIGH for 2 minutes.

Let the bowl and its contents sit inside the microwave for 1 minute to cool.

Stir the contents of the bowl with your heat-resistant spatula to see if the chips are melted. If you can stir the mixture smooth, you're ready to complete your candy. If you can't stir the mixture smooth, microwave it on HIGH in 20-second increments followed by a 1-minute standing time until you can stir it smooth.

Quickly add your broken pieces of pretzels

to the mixture in your bowl and stir them in.

Spread your Butterscotch Crunch Candy out in your prepared pan. Smooth it out on top with your heat-resistant spatula.

Hannah's 3rd Note: This is going to look lumpy. That's because of the pretzels.

Place the pan in the refrigerator, uncovered, for at least 2 hours.

Take the pan from the refrigerator, lift out the foil with the candy inside, and peel off the foil.

Cut your Butterscotch Crunch Candy into fudge-sized pieces.

Store the pieces in a covered container in the refrigerator.

Take the container out approximately 20 minutes before you want to serve your Butterscotch Crunch Candy.

Yield: 2 to 3 dozen pieces of delicious candy that both adults and children will love. The number of pieces depends, of course, on how large you cut them.

CASHEW CANDY ROLLS

Hannah's 1st Note: You do NOT need a candy thermometer to make this candy.

14-ounce can of sweetened condensed milk (**NOT evaporated milk**)

3 cups white baking chips (**18 ounces — see Hannah's 2nd Note**)

1 teaspoon salted butter

1 teaspoon vanilla extract

1/4 teaspoon salt

1 and 1/2 cups roughly chopped salted cashews (**measure AFTER chopping**)

Hannah's 2nd Note: If you use Ghirardelli chips, that's one 11-ounce bag and a little <u>more</u> than half of another. If you use Nestle Chips, that's one 12-ounce bag and half of another.

If you haven't already done so, chop the salted cashews into pieces about the size of coarse gravel. Then measure out one and a half cups. (**Cashews are easy to chop if you have a food processor and use the steel blade in an on-and-off motion, but a knife and a chopping board will work just fine.**)

Measure out the 3 cups of white chips. (**See Hannah's 2nd Note.**)

Open the can of sweetened condensed

milk and pour it into the bottom of a saucepan or a microwave-safe bowl that is large enough to also contain the white chips. Use a saucepan if you intend to melt this mixture on the stovetop. Use a microwave-safe bowl if you intend to melt the mixture in the microwave.

If you decided to use the stovetop, melt the mixture on LOW, stirring constantly, until the chips no longer maintain their shape.

If you decided to use the microwave, melt the mixture on HIGH. (*This will take approximately 80 seconds. Chips do retain their shape in the microwave, even after being melted, so let the bowl sit inside the microwave for approximately 1 minute before you try to stir the mixture smooth. If you cannot stir the mixture smooth, heat it on HIGH again in 20-second increments followed by a standing time of 1 minute, until the mixture can be stirred smooth.*)

When your mixture has melted smoothly, give it a final stir and then set it on top of a cold stovetop burner or on a thick towel on the kitchen counter to cool.

Let the mixture cool for 1 minute, and then mix in the butter, vanilla extract, and salt. (*Don't add the chopped cashews yet — they're for later when you make the candy rolls.*)

Hannah's 3rd Note: The week before the last Christmas, Lisa and I worked late making candy at The Cookie Jar. I was so tired that after I'd melted the chip mixture and let it cool on the counter for a minute, I dumped in the chopped cashews by mistake. I must have groaned out loud, because Lisa came over to look. She told me that was okay, got out a pan, lined it with foil, sprayed the foil with Pam, and put my mistake into the pan. It turned out to be all right after all. We kept it in the walk-in cooler overnight and the next morning we could cut it into pieces like fudge!

Put the saucepan or bowl in the refrigerator and chill the candy for 30 to 40 minutes.

Take the mixture out of the refrigerator and divide the candy in half. Place each half on a two-foot-long (*24 inches*) piece of wax paper.

Shape each half of the mixture into a roll with your fingers that's approximately a foot and a half long (*18 inches*) and about 1 and 1/2 inches thick.

Sprinkle the chopped cashews over the pieces of wax paper.

Roll the candy logs in the chopped cashews, coating them as evenly as you can. Press the cashews in slightly so that they'll stick to the outside of the rolls.

Wrap the finished logs in clean wax paper, twist the ends closed, and place them in the refrigerator for at least 2 hours to harden.

Hannah's 4th Note: You can store these candy rolls in the refrigerator for longer, if you don't want to serve them that day. Just take them out when you need them.

Cut your Cashew Candy Rolls into half-inch slices with a sharp knife. If the knife gets sticky, wash off the blade with cold running water, dry it off on a clean dish-towel, and resume cutting your candy.

Yield: Makes about 48 slices of delicious candy.

CHAPTER THIRTEEN

Hannah stood there in the cloakroom of the Corner Tavern, staring at the pair of light-brown boots at the end of the rack. They were Bonnie's boots. She recognized them. There were uneven patches of darker-colored brown on both of the boots from the sides of the soles all the way up to the ankles. There was no duct tape in sight, but it had probably lost its adhesive grip on the leather when the leather had gotten wet. But was the leather wet? Or was it simply discolored? Hannah had to know for certain.

She moved close enough to the boots to touch the area that looked wet. It was wet, very wet, so soaked that it had not yet dried out. The night that she'd seen Bonnie at the bar, the same night that Phyllis had been murdered, Bonnie had worn her soaked boots inside the Corner Tavern and then she'd changed to the only dry footwear she'd had in her car, her red tennis shoes and a pair of Gil's argyle socks. But the pair of wet boots didn't necessarily mean that Bonnie had anything to do with Phyllis's murder. Bonnie might have walked through some deep snow before she got to the Corner Tavern, realized that her boots were wet when she arrived, and carried her tennis shoes inside to put them on in the cloakroom.

A warning bell in Hannah's mind clanged insistently. Mike needed to know about Bonnie's boots. She really should take a photo and send it to Mike. She'd promised to keep him informed of anything she'd found that could relate to the murder. And even though she didn't believe that Bonnie had anything to do with it, she had an obligation to share this information with Mike.

Hannah pulled out her phone, took a photo of the boots, and tried to remember what her niece Tracey had taught her about attaching a photo to a text message. She titled the photo Bonnie's Boots and hit the proper series of buttons to send the photo to Mike.

"Yes!" Hannah said out loud when the attachment worked. And then she frowned. She'd sent the photo, but she hadn't typed a text message explaining anything about it. Hannah knew that she should send another text to explain, but it was getting late and she still had to stop to take the soup and candy to Bonnie before she would be free to join Michelle and Lonnie for lunch. She could always text Mike later.

For a long moment, Hannah debated whether she should take the boots with her and give them to Bonnie. But Bonnie had left them here and she probably didn't want them back. Bonnie's fix with duct tape had probably worked just fine on shoveled sidewalks and plowed streets, but it was quite obvious that deep snow had rendered the repair useless.

Had Bonnie killed Phyllis? She'd had the opportunity and her boots were wet, but that proved nothing conclusive. There could be a perfectly reasonable explanation for the wet boots. Bonnie was a pillar of the community, a deeply religious person who was active in her church, and a woman who worked tirelessly for the good of the Lake Eden community. Hannah was almost positive that there was a reasonable explanation for Bonnie's wet boots. She would ask when she took Bonnie the soup and the candy.

Hannah opened the front porch door and stepped inside. It was common practice for Lake Edenites to leave their front porches unlocked during the winter so that visitors could step in to get out of the wind or the snow. Hannah walked to the inside door and knocked, but there was no answer. She listened for a moment, but all she heard from inside was the sound of a television game show with buzzers and bells, and the excited voices of the contestants. If Bonnie had fallen asleep watching television, Hannah didn't want to wake her. Sick people needed their rest. But what if Bonnie hadn't fallen asleep? What if she'd taken a turn for the worse and she was too ill to get up to answer Hannah's knock at the door?

Tentatively, Hannah tried the doorknob. It turned and she pushed it open an inch or two. The enthusiastic utterances of the daytime game show host were louder, but she also heard a rhythmic creaking noise that she could not identify.

Hannah glanced at the coatrack as she hung up her winter things in the front hallway. Bonnie's coat was hanging there, along with a warm scarf, and a knit hat with earflaps and a tassel on the top. It was four degrees below zero today. Hannah had glanced at the indoor-outdoor thermometer that hung outside the kitchen window at The Cookie Jar before she'd left. That was much too cold to go anywhere without a coat, or a scarf, or a hat. Bonnie was home.

Uncertain but determined, Hannah opened the door all the way and stepped inside. She stood there for a moment, not sure what to do next, and then she hung her parka on the coatrack and headed toward the sound of the television set. She called out once, but Bonnie didn't answer. She'd leave the soup and the candy if she found Bonnie asleep, and call Gil at the school to tell him they were there.

The television was in the den. She remembered that from the last time she'd been invited to one of Bonnie's home meetings. Hannah hurried down the hallway, stepped into the den, and found Bonnie there. Bonnie was not asleep. She was sitting in a rocking chair with an afghan around her shoulders, and she was rocking back and forth.

It didn't take more than a moment to realize that the creaking noise had come from the rocking chair. Bonnie's eyes were closed, and Hannah approached quietly. "Bonnie?" she said softly. "It's Hannah. I brought you some soup because Danielle said you were sick."

Bonnie's eyes opened. They appeared huge and unfocused. "Hannah?" Bonnie asked.

"Yes. It's me, Bonnie. Would you like me

to heat you some soup? Michelle made it."

Bonnie's expression changed to one of puzzlement. "Michelle?" she asked.

It was clear that Bonnie was not in control of her faculties, and Hannah proceeded carefully. "Michelle is my youngest sister. It's Hannah, Hannah Swensen. You recognize me, don't you, Bonnie?"

"Oh, Hannah. Of course I recognize you. But what are you doing here? It's a school day. Why aren't you in class?"

Something was wrong, very wrong, and Hannah knew it. Bonnie was either drugged or still half asleep because the normally cognizant woman that Hannah admired was slipping in and out of reality. Perhaps it would be best to stick with everyday questions at first.

"Are you hungry?" Hannah asked.

"I . . . I don't know. I could be, I think."

"All right then. I'll go heat the chicken soup that I brought." Hannah stopped and evaluated Bonnie's blank expression. "Is that all right, Bonnie?"

"Oh, yes. It's fine. Gil should be home and he'll be hungry. He always comes home for lunch on school days." Bonnie stopped and took a deep breath. "This is a school day, isn't it?"

"Yes, it is. I'll be right back, Bonnie."

"Oh, good. I like you, Hannah, but don't interfere. Never interfere in anything that doesn't concern you. My mother told me that, and it was some of the best advice I ever got. I just wish I'd followed it sooner."

Bonnie smiled once, and then her expression faded again to a perfectly blank stare. It reminded Hannah of teddy bears in an arcade booth, waiting to go home with their lucky winners. "Are you sure you're okay alone?"

"I'm always alone. Everyone is. We're born alone and we die alone. It's a fact of life."

Hannah shivered. Bonnie's voice was devoid of inflection, almost like the recorded voice of the time of day on the telephone. "I suppose you're right, Bonnie," she said, attempting to smile as she went off to the kitchen to heat the soup.

It only took two minutes to heat the soup in the microwave. Hannah found a soup bowl in the cupboard and returned to the den. "Here you are, Bonnie," she said, placing the bowl and spoon on the table next to Bonnie. "This should make you feel better."

"Nothing will make me feel better until I go," Bonnie said, not even reaching out for the soup. "She was my daughter, you know."

Hannah's mind took a huge leap, and suddenly she thought she knew exactly what

Bonnie meant. "Phyllis," she said, recalling Danielle's comment that Bonnie had regarded Phyllis as her daughter.

"Yes. She went bad, Hannah . . . horribly bad. She forgot my lessons, and she wouldn't listen when I tried to correct her. She said she wasn't in school, and she didn't have to listen to me. And then she pushed me away!"

Hannah felt a cold chill run through her as Bonnie's eyes began to glitter. Her mind was teeming with questions, but she didn't want to ask them for fear it would cut off the flow of Bonnie's words.

"I taught her what to do, how to act like a lady, but she reverted to type. She tempted men and used them for her own gain. Mayor Bascomb was weak. He couldn't help himself when she threw herself at him. And she was going to do it again. I saw that lunch bag, and I knew."

Bonnie rocked a little faster and the speed of her speech increased along with the creaking. "Herb would have fallen under her spell. I knew that and I had to stop her. Men are weak. Except for Gil. Gil tried to save me. And he did . . . for years and years. Gil is my savior. Gil is my rock. I put my trust in him and he will not fail me."

Hannah was silent. She wasn't sure what

to say, but she knew she had to say something. She reached into her pocket, clicked the voice record button on her smartphone and said, "I found your boots, Bonnie. And now I know that you killed Phyllis."

Bonnie looked up at her again with those big, unfocused eyes. "But you see, I had to. She wouldn't listen to me when I tried to correct her, to set her on the right path again. She laughed at me. I kept trying. I reminded her of what it meant to be a lady and she told me to shut up, but I persevered. She could not get away from me, from the truth. She tried, but I followed her."

"Down into the ditch," Hannah said, knowing she was right.

"Yes. Yes, down in the ditch. And she slipped and fell."

The rocker slowed. And then it stopped. Bonnie's eyes attempted to focus on Hannah. "You won't tell Gil, will you? He sees the good in everyone. Do you have any idea how hard it is to live with someone who sees the good in everyone?"

Again, Hannah wasn't sure how to answer so she changed the subject, bringing it back to the murder. "I know why you killed Phyllis. But tell me how you did it. I want to understand."

"She did not suffer. I made sure of that. I

found a branch. And I stood above her and I stamped her out. She was evil and it was my duty. You must stamp out evil wherever you find it. The angel helped me do it. The angel guided my arms. You know the angel, don't you, Hannah?"

Hannah took a wild leap into the morass of a twisted mind. "The angel of death?" she asked.

"Yes! I knew you'd understand. You're a good person, Hannah, and I know that you'll be rewarded in the afterlife. The angel will help me with you, too. I'm sorry, Hannah, but I can't let you live. I can't let you tell Gil what I've done. He'd never understand!"

"Maybe he would," Hannah said quickly, hoping to keep Bonnie talking.

"I'd like to believe that, but I know it isn't so. You must go first and then me. We'll take the journey together, one right after the other."

Hannah thought fast. "I'll just heat some soup for Gil first. I'll do it right now and come back."

"No," Bonnie said, and her tone was as flat as the flagstone on the front of the fireplace in Bonnie's den. "You must stay right here so that I can release you from this earthly plane. Gil will be home soon, and the deed must be done before he comes home."

As Hannah watched in horror, Bonnie drew a gun from beneath her afghan and pointed it directly at Hannah. "It won't hurt, Hannah. I'd never hurt you. You're my friend, and we can be together in the hereafter."

Hannah knew she had to say something to stop Bonnie from using the gun. Her breakdown could be the result of guilt over the murder she'd committed, or she could be out of her mind from the fever that accompanied her cold. Hannah didn't really care what had caused Bonnie's mind to snap. She just knew that she had to get out of the den. And fast!

"Wait just a moment, Bonnie," Hannah said, as calmly as she could. "Give me a little time to heat more soup. It's comfort food, and Gil will need something to comfort himself when he sees both us here."

Bonnie's expression changed. She looked a bit thoughtful. "Do you really think so?"

"I do. It will be a shock, Bonnie. And everyone knows that you should give something warm, something comforting to people who are in shock."

"I've heard that. And you're right, Hannah." Bonnie nodded, but then her eyes narrowed. "But will you come back here so that I can release you?"

Hannah heard the sound of the front door opening, and she answered quickly so that it would mask the sound of the door. "Oh, yes. I'll be back. You're right, Bonnie. It'll only take a minute or two and then I'll be back with you."

And then Gil was standing in the doorway of the den, an expression of disbelief on his face as he stared at his wife with the gun in her hand. "Bonnie?" he said in the calm, friendly voice that Hannah assumed he used with his troubled students. "What are you doing, darling?"

"Don't you see?" Bonnie responded, turning toward him. "I have to release her, Gil. She knows I killed Phyllis. And then we can go, too. Together. Isn't that right, darling?"

"Yes, of course," Gil said. "Just let me think for a moment, dear." And then, when Bonnie's arm lowered slightly, Gil rushed toward her and grabbed the gun before Bonnie could raise it again. They tussled for a moment, as Hannah stood there, frozen. The struggle seemed to last forever, and Hannah's feet seemed glued to the spot. And then Gil forced Bonnie's arm up so that the barrel of the gun was pointing toward the ceiling.

"Run, Hannah!" he shouted at her. "Run for help!"

Gil's words served to release her and Hannah didn't waste any time. She ran out of the den and into the hallway, headlong toward the front door. She didn't stop to grab her coat, she just fled as fast as she could. She pulled the heavy inner door open, expecting to run to her truck, but she found herself engulfed in the arms of someone wearing a sheriff's department uniform. It was Mike and she'd never been so glad to see anyone in her whole life!

"Hannah!" Mike exclaimed. "Where's Bonnie?"

"The den!" Hannah managed to gasp out.

"Michelle's in the cruiser. Take her and get out of here. Now!"

"Bonnie's got a gun. Gil grabbed her arm, and . . ."

The sound of a gunshot drowned out any further explanation Hannah could give him. Mike drew his gun, motioned to Lonnie, who was standing behind him, and both men raced for the den.

Hannah knew she should go, but she couldn't, not without finding out what had happened. She drew a deep, shaking breath and turned around to follow Mike and Lonnie to the den. She arrived at the doorway just in time to see the gun on the floor next to the rocker, and Gil cradling his wife's body in his arms.

"I shot her," he said to Mike and Lonnie. "She was going to kill Hannah. You have to arrest me. I killed my darling wife."

CHAPTER FOURTEEN

Hannah stared out of the passenger window at scenery she didn't see. The image of Gil holding Bonnie's body in his arms was too fresh in her mind.

"Are you all right, Hannah?" Michelle asked, as she pulled the cookie truck into Hannah's parking space at the condo.

"I don't know," Hannah answered truthfully. "It's like . . . too much for my mind to process. I can't take it all in. It's not right, Michelle. It never should have happened this way. Nothing's right!"

"Mike said that you were in shock and you have to rest. You haven't gotten a good night's sleep since this whole thing started. You're overloaded, overtired, and completely stressed. You need to stretch out on your bed and nap with Moishe until Mike gets here."

"But I should call . . ."

"No one," Michelle interrupted her. "You

should call no one. You're in no shape to talk right now. You've always taken care of me, and now it's my turn to take care of you."

"I . . . I'm not sure . . ." Hannah's voice trailed off. Michelle was right. She was so terribly, terribly tired.

"Come on, Hannah," Michelle walked around the back of the cookie truck and pulled open Hannah's door. "Let's go upstairs and see Moishe. That'll make you feel better."

"Not if I have to catch him," Hannah said, eliciting a laugh from Michelle.

"I'll catch him," Michelle promised, leading the way up the covered outside staircase. "And I'll unlock the door, too. I want you to go in, walk straight to the bedroom, and take a nap. If you do, I guarantee you'll feel better by the time Mike comes to take your statement."

"Yes," Hannah said, and then she gave her sister a hug. "Thank you, Michelle."

She could see him at the foot of her bed. Hannah stared at him for a moment and then she sat up. "Dad?"

"Yes, Honey-bear. It's me. I'm back and I'm here to be the Ghost of Christmas Future."

"There is no future for Bonnie."

"I know. That's unfortunate. But there is a future for you, Hannah. It's a happy future, and I need to show it to you. And I need to show you something from Lisa's future, too. Don't tell her. It's going to be a Christmas surprise."

As Hannah watched, the movie screen materialized and images began to appear. The first image was of Lisa's house as a sporty red car drove up to park in the driveway. It was an older model but beautifully restored with fresh paint and new tires. As she watched, Herb placed a huge red and green bow on top of the car, and Hannah knew that it must be a Christmas present. Then Herb walked to the front door of the house and went inside.

A moment later, Lisa followed Herb outside. She saw the car and blinked and stared, as if she couldn't believe her eyes. And then, when Herb handed Lisa the keys, Lisa threw her arms around him and kissed him.

The scene changed. The whole family was sitting around a beautifully decorated Christmas tree in her mother's living room. They were exchanging presents on Christmas Day, and Delores handed Hannah a long, flat package in gold paper with little candy canes printed all over it. There was a tag on the front that read, *From Dad and Uncle Ed.* Hannah took off the ribbon and bow very carefully and handed them to her mother. Delores saved things like that. Then she took off the paper and stared down at the beautifully restored and refinished board inside. Someone had carved two names into the wood in childish block letters. One name was Ed and the other was Lars.

"Your uncle Ed was lucky," her father's voice said. "He only had to carve two letters. I had to carve four on the ladder we used to get up into our treehouse. I'm glad you kept our ladder, Honey-bear. And I'm glad your mother remembered what I told her about it."

Hannah's mouth dropped open. So *that* was why Delores had wanted the old ladder that had almost caused Lisa to tumble to the floor. She'd removed the board where Hannah's Uncle Ed and father had carved their names as boys and restored it as a plaque for Hannah.

The screen went dark and Hannah sighed. She was sorry the glimpse into the future was over. But her father was still here and she concentrated on the form at the foot of her bed. It was beginning to undulate and fade, and she knew that he was about to leave her.

"Dad!" she called out to him. "Will you come back, Dad?"

"I'm always here, Honey-bear. I always will be. And I promise that I'll always give you a kiss on Christmas morning, just the way I used to do when I woke you up to tell you that Santa had come."

Hannah opened her mouth to ask another question, but the amorphous form that had been her father changed into wisps of sparkling gold that floated up to the ceiling and then beyond.

"He's gone," she said to Moishe. "Dad's gone, but he promised he'd kiss me on Christmas morning."

Moishe began to purr and then he licked her hand. And Hannah gave him a scratch behind his ears, something he loved, and that made him purr even louder.

"Hannah?" a voice called her out of her half-awake state. "Mike's here. I'll give him some coffee and a couple of the Cherry Shortbread Bar Cookies I made. How do you feel?"

Michelle appeared in the doorway and Hannah smiled at her. "I feel good. You and Mike were right. Sleep was exactly what I needed."

CHERRY SHORTBREAD
BAR COOKIES

Preheat oven to 350 degrees F., rack in the middle position

The Crust and Topping Mixture:

3 cups all-purpose flour (*pack it down in the cup when you measure it*)

3/4 cup powdered (*confectioner's*) sugar (*don't sift unless it's got big lumps*)

1/2 teaspoon salt

1/2 teaspoon cinnamon

1/4 teaspoon grated nutmeg (*freshly grated is best*)

1 and 1/2 cups slightly softened butter (*3 sticks, 12 ounces, 3/4 pound*)

The Filling:

1 can (*21 ounces*) cherry pie filling (*I used Comstock*)

FIRST STEP: Use a fork to mix flour, powdered sugar, salt, cinnamon, and nutmeg together in a bowl.

Mix in the softened butter until the mixture forms little nuggets about the size of coarse gravel.

(*You can also do this in a food processor using cold butter cut into chunks, layered with the dry ingredients. Process with the steel blade in an on-and-off motion until it resembles coarse gravel.*)

Spray a 9-inch by 13-inch pan (*That's a standard-sized rectangular cake pan*) with Pam or another non-stick cooking spray.

Spread approximately HALF of the crust and topping mixture (*approx. 2 and 1/2 cups*) into the pan you prepared.

Bake at 350 degrees F. for 15 minutes. Remove the pan from the oven, but DON'T TURN OFF THE OVEN! You'll be using it again in just a few minutes and you won't have time to preheat it again.

Let the crust cool for 5 minutes.

SECOND STEP: Open the can of cherry pie filling and pour it out into a bowl. Use a knife to cut the cherries into smaller pieces.

Spread the cherry pie filling over the top of the crust you just baked.

Sprinkle the cherry pie filling with the other half of the crust and topping mixture.

Gently press the topping down with a wide, metal spatula.

Bake the bar cookies for another 30 to 35 minutes, or until the top is golden. Remove the pan from the oven, turn off the oven, and place the pan on a cold stovetop burner or a wire rack.

Cool the Cherry Shortbread Bar Cookies thoroughly.

When the pan is cool to the touch, cut the bar cookies into brownie-sized bars while they're right there in the pan.

If you want to be a little fancy, sprinkle your bar cookies with a little extra powdered sugar.

Cover the pan with foil and refrigerate your cut bar cookies until you're ready to serve them. Then use a small spatula to remove them and put them on a pretty platter.

You can also serve these bar cookies as a dessert if you cut them into larger pieces and warm them in dessert dishes in the microwave.

As a finishing touch, place a dollop of sweetened, whipped cream, OR a scoop of vanilla ice cream on top.

EPILOGUE

"Hannah?" Ross put down his empty coffee cup. "Yes, Ross."

"I have a couple of questions for you."

"Okay." Hannah mentally prepared herself for some tough questions like *Do you really believe that you saw your father?* or *Don't you think that your subconscious was staging all these dreams because of the play the Lake Eden Players were doing, and your mind was working to form inferences from all the information you'd received during the day?* "What would you like to know?" she asked him.

"I know that Lisa has a red car. Did Herb restore it and give it to her last Christmas?"

"Yes, he did. He told us that he worked late every night out at Cyril Murphy's garage to get it ready by Christmas."

"And that's why Lisa thought he was going out on her?"

"Yes. And the reason Mike cleared Herb was because Cyril was helping Herb on the night that Phyllis was murdered. But Mike couldn't tell me that because Herb wanted it to be a secret so that Lisa would have a Christmas surprise."

Ross smiled. "Was she surprised?"

"And how!" Hannah used one of her favorite Minnesota expressions. "Lisa nearly had a cow when she saw that gorgeous car!"

"How about your present, the one your mother gave you?"

"It was a board from Dad's old ladder with Dad and Uncle Ed's names on it."

"And you pretended to be surprised?"

Hannah smiled. "I did."

"Is that the same plaque that you have hanging in your hallway?"

"It is. I love that plaque. There's no way you can know your parents as children, and sometimes it's nice to be reminded that they were really kids, just like you."

"A lot happened in Lake Eden last Christmas," Ross said, and he looked thoughtful. "Maybe you'd better not make those chocolate caramels again . . . just in case, I mean."

Hannah laughed. "We haven't made them since, but it's silly to think they're bad luck, isn't it?"

"Rationally, yes. Of course it is. And of course I want you to make them. I missed out last year. But you've got to promise me one thing."

"What's that?"

"You've got to promise that you won't find another body right before Christmas this year."

"But how can I promise something like that? Mike says I have slaydar. I don't go looking for murder victims, but I seem to find them more often than other people do."

"That's true." Ross gave a little sigh. "I know it's silly, Hannah. And I know it could happen whether you promise, or not. But . . . will you promise anyway?"

Hannah smiled at him. "If it'll make you feel better, I promise," she said.

CHRISTMAS CARAMEL
MURDER RECIPE INDEX

BAKING CONVERSION CHART

These conversions are approximate, but they'll work just fine for Hannah Swensen's recipes.

VOLUME:

U.S.	Metric
1/2 teaspoon	2 milliliters
1 teaspoon	5 milliliters
1 Tablespoon	15 milliliters
1/4 cup	50 milliliters
1/3 cup	75 milliliters
1/2 cup	125 milliliters
3/4 cup	175 milliliters
1 cup	1/4 liter

WEIGHT:

U.S.	Metric
1 ounce	28 grams
1 pound	454 grams

OVEN TEMPERATURE:

Degrees Fahrenheit   325 degrees F.
Degrees Centigrade   165 degrees C.
British (Regulo) Gas Mark 3

Degrees Fahrenheit   350 degrees F.
Degrees Centigrade   175 degrees C.
British (Regulo) Gas Mark 4

Degrees Fahrenheit   375 degrees F.
Degrees Centigrade   190 degrees C.
British (Regulo) Gas Mark 5

Note: Hannah's rectangular sheet cake pan, 9 inches by 13 inches, is approximately 23 centimeters by 32.5 centimeters.

ABOUT THE AUTHOR

Joanne Fluke is the *New York Times* best-selling author of twenty Hannah Swensen mysteries. The first novel in the series (*Chocolate Chip Cookie Murder*) premiered as *Murder, She Baked: A Chocolate Chip Cookie Mystery* on the Hallmark Movies & Mysteries Channel. Like Hannah Swensen, Joanne Fluke was born and raised in a small town in rural Minnesota, but now lives in Southern California. Please visit her online at www.joannefluke.com